TEST OF THE DRAGON

A DRAGON RIDERS OF ELANTIA NOVEL

JASMINE WALT

Copyright © 2023, Jasmine Walt. All rights reserved. Published by Dynamo Press.

This novel is a work of fiction. All characters, places, and incidents described in this publication are used fictitiously, or are entirely fictional. No part of this publication may be reproduced or transmitted, in any form or by any means, except by an authorized retailer, or with written permission of the publisher. Inquiries may be addressed via email to jasmine@jasminewalt.com.

If you want to be notified when Jasmine's next novel is released and get access to exclusive contests, giveaways, and freebies, sign up for her mailing list at www.jasminewalt.com. Your email address will never be shared and you can unsubscribe at any time.

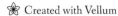 Created with Vellum

ONE

"*Zara, I think we're here!*"

Lessie's excitement penetrated the fog in my head, waking me from a deep slumber. Yawning, I stirred in Tavarian's arms and blinked the sleep from my eyes, then glanced over the side of my dragon's back to get a good look at the terrain. My heart jumped in my chest at the sight before me—we were flying over the middle of the ocean, its deep blue waves shimmering beneath us. Dawn crested the skyline, backlighting the huge island just ahead so that it looked like a giant sea turtle rising out of the waves.

Polyba. We were finally here.

"*Looks like it,*" I told her with a smile as I leaned back against Tavarian. His solid chest was a comfort, and as he tightened his arms around me, I was reminded just how much things had changed between us. Once, he'd been a target, a high and mighty dragon rider lord I'd had to steal from in order to protect my shop.

Now he was my friend, my lover, my partner.

And together, we were going to save our nation.

"It will be nice to finally get the chance to rest," I said aloud to both of them. "Although I suppose that depends on the state of the camp when we arrive. Do you think Jallis and Rhia will have settled everyone in by now?"

"They should have arrived several days ago," Tavarian pointed out. "But then again, it depends on how hostile the environment is, and whether or not any natives live there. I don't know much about the island beyond what Rhiannon told us."

The last time we'd all been together, Rhia had disclosed that her dragon, Ykos, knew of a secret weapon hidden on this island. Apparently, one of his ancestors had been partnered with a rider from another dragon rider family, and that family had owned a secret estate on Polyba where they'd kept quite a few treasures. Unfortunately, that was hundreds of years ago, and the estate was likely abandoned. We had no idea if anyone lived there.

"Oh, there are definitely natives on the island," Lessie said, and I sat up straighter in the saddle, alarmed at the sudden change in her voice. *"I can see at least two settlements from this side of the island."*

"Two settlements?" Tavarian asked when I told him what Lessie had said. "Where?"

I slipped my goggles on and zoomed in on the island. As we got closer, more of the terrain came into view, and my stomach sank a little. I'd hoped for a lush, fertile isle, perhaps with forests and plains full of wildlife, but instead we were greeted with rocky coasts and hilly terrain. The mountains, amongst which skinny goats foraged, sported a few trees here and there, but mostly they were covered with bushes that belonged to arid climes. As I swept my gaze from one end of the island to the other, I spotted two clusters of ramshackle huts that might be villages located on opposite ends of the island.

"Let's do a flyover," I told Lessie. "We need to get a better lay of the land and figure out where the others have made camp." For all I knew, the natives were friendly, welcoming people, but I'd been through enough recently that I wasn't willing to take that chance.

Lessie nodded and angled her body downward, dipping low enough for us to get a clear view of the island without exposing us to arrows or any other projectiles the locals might have. Circling around, we found a third settlement toward the north of the island, nestled near some of the highest peaks. We also found an ancient, crumbling estate located closer to the center of the island, and half a dozen or so isolated farms scattered about. The coasts themselves were too rocky and inhospitable for ships to land, but we did find two small harbors near the settlements, and some roads that amounted to little more than goat paths.

"This is disheartening," Tavarian said, his voice tight with worry. "An island like this would be hard-pressed to provide enough resources to sustain two settlements, never mind three. And then there is our own party to contend with..."

As if on cue, two dragons rose from a valley toward the east side of the island. Lessie roared in excitement as she caught sight of Kiethara, the female ruby red dragon she'd befriended after we'd broken the dragons out from their Zallabarian prison.

Her rider was Halldor Savin, the hotheaded, red-haired captain I'd taken quite a liking to. The other dragon was Ragor, Ullion's dragon, and I couldn't help but smile in relief as they greeted us.

"Commandant!" Savin cried, using the honorary title my fellow soldiers had bestowed upon me. I was a private by rank, but after freeing the dragon riders from Zallabar's clutches, they'd felt I deserved a better title. "Lord Tavarian! Welcome back. I take it your mission was successful?"

"It was," I called back, noting the curiosity in his eyes. He didn't press, but I was sure he and everyone else at the camp were wondering what took so long for us to join them. Would I need to explain to them about the dragon god threat? I wasn't looking forward to that at all.

"You've made it just in time for breakfast." The corner of Ullion's mouth curved into a sardonic smile, but he didn't say more than that. "Please, come with us and we'll lead you to the camp."

We followed the two riders to a second estate, smaller than the first one we'd seen but in better condition. Tucked into a valley, it provided some security, and the estate had a paved courtyard where the dragons could land safely without worrying about the thorny bushes that liberally dotted the island. There was also a clearing to the west of the estate where the dragons were pastured, large enough for the hundred or so dragons we'd brought but too small for them to run about freely. Most of them were curled up in the grass, resting, and some of the tension slid off my shoulders as I watched them. At least they were finally getting some peace after going through such a terrible ordeal. As we touched down, I expected to feel some sense of relief, but the heavy mood in the air only increased the dismay in my stomach.

"We've managed to burn away a large clearing to the west of the estate," Ullion said as we dismounted. "Lessie can rest there while we bring you up to speed."

"All right." I patted Lessie's side, then divested her of the saddle and luggage strapped to her body. The two riders immediately stepped forward and took our belongings before Tavarian and I could pick them up, then led us through the remnants of an iron gate and into the manor house ahead.

"Zara!" Jallis and Rhia jumped to their feet as we were ushered into what looked to be a great hall—a once-grand room with cracked walls and moldy remnants of carpet. Rusted pieces of metal were tucked into the corner, likely once part of a spectacular chandelier. Everyone was gathered here, sitting cross-legged on the floor in groups of ten as they ate off plates that looked to be fashioned from pieces of stone and tile, but they all rose at the sight of us. Their faces brightened as they cheered at our arrival, but that didn't reassure me—I'd seen the glum looks on their faces before they'd noticed me.

Rhia darted forward, the first to reach me. "I'm so relieved you're back," she said as she threw her arms around me. "How did everything go?" she whispered in my ear. "Did you manage to recover the piece of heart?"

"I did." At Rhia's reminder, I was suddenly aware of the weight of the pouch strapped to my belt. It held one of the five pieces of Zakyiar's heart—the dragon god had come to our world over two thousand years ago and nearly destroyed it. "I'll tell you all about it later, when we have some time to catch up."

Rhia nodded, pulling away, and I looked up to see Jallis standing nearby. The warm smile on his face held no trace of the anger or resentment that had built steadily between us since our time in the military together, but nevertheless, the lines of his face showed signs of tension.

"Come sit down, Zara," he said, instantly reading the questions in my eyes. "We can bring you up to speed while we eat."

Tavarian and I joined them on the floor, and we were served a frugal meal of olives, fish, and flatbread. We were seated with Jallis, Rhia, Halldor, Kade, Ullion, Daria, and two other captains whose names I didn't remember. They all took turns reporting to me on the state of the camp, though Rhia and Jallis did most of the talking.

"I'd hoped that we could have everything settled by the time you and Tavarian arrived," Rhia said as she nibbled on a bit of flatbread. Now that the introductions were over, I noticed the shadows under her eyes. "Unfortunately, we've been running into problems since day one."

"There's a lot less food on the island than we'd hoped for," Jallis said. "Thankfully, we still had rations from Tavarian's airship, but we've burned through those already, aside from a few sacks of flour we've been using to make the bread. We've been subsisting mostly off fish and olives, and the occasional rabbit we catch in the snares. The airship has gone back to Warosia to purchase some more supplies, but we're running low on gold, so I'm not sure how long that's going to last. We need to figure out how to grow our own food."

"I may be able to procure more funds," Tavarian said. "We can use the money to buy seeds to grow crops, though we'll be limited to whatever can grow in this dry soil. Have you tried going to the locals for help?"

"The locals have been anything but helpful," Halldor growled, his face turning red. "The other day they sold us three sheep, and it turned out one of them had been poisoned! Thankfully Kiethara's stomach is made of stern stuff, but she was sick for a whole day and night before she finally recovered. It's taken everything we've got to keep our dragons from going after the natives in retaliation."

"To be fair," Ullion said, clearing his throat, "the poisoning was not entirely unprovoked."

I raised an eyebrow. "What does that mean?"

The riders exchanged uneasy glances. "A few of the dragons may have decided they were tired of fish and decided to go hunting instead. They may also have decided to go after the natives' goat herds."

Tavarian scrubbed a hand over his face as I let out a groan. "Great. So we're trespassing on their island and stealing their property. No wonder they love us."

"They could be a little more understanding of our predicament," Daria snapped. "It's not like we want to be here. Why does this island have to be so inhospitable?"

"It's my fault," Rhia said, her shoulders hunching inward a little. My heart ached a little at the guilty expression on her face. "I'm the one who told us to come here in the first place."

Kade's cheeks turned pink. "I didn't mean it like that, Rhia."

"No, he didn't." Halldor flashed Kade an annoyed look, then

took Rhia's hand in his. I raised an eyebrow at the way his expression softened when he looked at her. "You couldn't have known about the natives, or the island's topography. And although we may be dealing with some frustrating setbacks, at least we don't have the Zallabarians breathing down our necks right now."

"Maybe, but the secret weapon doesn't even seem to be here," Rhia said. Her eyes met mine, and my heart sank a little more at the defeated look in them. "We went to the other estate on the island, but it's been looted. There wasn't even a piece of broken pottery to be found."

"That doesn't mean the item isn't there," I said, trying to stay optimistic. "We'll go back tomorrow and look again with my treasure sense. Besides, even if it's not there, it's likely somewhere on this island. One way or the other, we'll find it."

If it exists. The voice of doubt echoed in my head, but I shoved it down. We'd cross that bridge when we came to it.

TWO

After lunch, I walked around the base with Rhia and Tavarian to get a better lay of the land. Though I kept my treasure sense dialed to the highest setting, we found little of value—a few semi-precious gems buried in the dirt, but no artifacts or treasure.

"Oh well," Rhia said when we finished our inspection. "I suppose an island like this has always been too poor for much treasure. Anything of value here was probably carted off by the natives."

"If that's the case," I said, "then they might have found the weapon at the other estate and taken it for themselves." I shuddered at the thought of the locals having access to anything that was as powerful as Ykos's ancestor had hinted at.

"If they did have the weapon, they would have likely used it on us to drive us off," Tavarian pointed out. "No, it is more likely that it was hidden very well on the estate, possibly by magic. Between the two of us, we should be able to ferret it out."

We turned to head back to the manor, when suddenly Rhia's face brightened. "Look!" She pointed to the sky. "The crew is back!"

My heart lifted at the sight of Tavarian's airship. They would have provisions on board, sorely needed at camp just now, and extra spaces to sleep as well.

"Watch out!" Halldor's warning echoed through the valley as he raced out of the manor. "There are men hidden in the bushes, waiting to attack!"

"Where?"

An arrow whizzed through the air from a clump of bushes up on the hillside, answering my question. The first arrow missed its mark, but the second one struck the balloon, and soon it was peppered with holes. The ship careened wildly to the side as it fought to get out of range, and my heart dropped into my shoes as it began to plummet.

"Lessie!" I cried, but she was already on it, darting forward with Kadryn and another dragon on her heels. The three of them launched themselves into the sky, buoying the airship with their big bodies before it could crash into the side of the manor. Arrows bounced harmlessly off their sides as they carried the ship to safety.

"Can we get those bastards?" Rhia growled in a voice that was quite unlike her own. The rage sparkling in her caramel brown eyes would have startled me if I hadn't felt exactly the same.

"They've likely already run off," Tavarian said. "But I can provide a shield while we go check out the area."

Tavarian waved his arm, making the air around us shimmer

as if a heat wave surrounded us. The gentle breeze wafting around us disappeared, as if four walls insulated us. "These should keep out any arrows," he said as we ran toward the location from which the arrows had come.

"Handy trick," Rhia said. "Would have been helpful to have something like that to protect the ship."

Tavarian said nothing to that, but I could tell from the subtle tightening around his eyes that Rhia's words had found their mark. I knew she hadn't intentionally been trying to criticize Tavarian, but as a man who was used to being in charge of important missions, having so little control over his own magic had to be frustrating as hell. I wished that there was a mage who could teach him, but Tavarian had been forced to keep the secret of his lineage for a long time, so he'd never had the benefit of formal training.

Maybe when we were finally settled and in relative safety, Tavarian would find the time to seek out a mage for proper training. But for now, we would make do with what we had.

We found the area where the locals had staged their attack fairly easily—one of the bushes was badly singed, likely by a false start with the arrows. I quickly found a trail of retreating footsteps and went after them with Rhia while Tavarian went ahead to check on the ship. But the locals knew what they were doing, and we lost their trail in no time.

Disheartened, Rhia and I returned to the base, where Tavarian was talking with the ship's captain. The crew looked a bit shaken from the ordeal, but they were already in motion, working with the dragon riders to unload the contents.

"What's the damage like?" I asked the captain.

"The ship itself took some minor damage to the hull," the captain said. "Much less than it would have if we'd crash-landed, but the dragons could only take us down so easily." He glanced toward Lessie and the others, who had formed a perimeter around the ship and were guarding it fiercely. "Thank the skies that they caught us in time. Anyway, the balloon itself is the biggest issue. We can repair the hull just fine, but we'll need special cloth to fix the balloon, and we don't have any to spare on board."

I frowned at Tavarian. "Shouldn't all ships come with a backup balloon?"

He shook his head. "A second balloon would be too heavy. However, all ships are supposed to carry spare material to patch the balloon. Why don't we have any left?"

"We used it up already," the captain said guiltily. "The original was damaged in flight, and we had to evacuate the country before I had time to order more patches."

"Damn." Tavarian scrubbed a hand over his jaw, which was dotted liberally with stubble. The beard growth made him look more rugged, especially coupled with his black hair, which was currently loose and wild around his face after the long flight we'd yet to clean up from. "Well, surely we must be able to get that cloth from Warosia."

"We can," the captain confirmed. "But we'll need to send a dragon."

Tavarian was still discussing logistics when Halldor came up beside my elbow, looking out of breath. "Commandant," he began. "I'm so sorry. This is all my fault."

I frowned. "How could this be your fault? You're not working with the natives, are you?"

"No, of course not," he said, his face flushing. "But if I was paying closer attention, I would have sensed those men approaching earlier. My talent allows me to sense how many people are in a given radius," he explained. "I was often put on watches during my military career for that reason."

"Really?" The fog of depression lifted from my mind, my interest piqued. "How large of a radius?"

"About two square miles," he said. "I've been trying to extend it, but it seems I can only go so far."

"Tavarian might be able to help you," I said. When Halldor looked puzzled, I explained, "He used his magic to enhance my own talent not long after I came to Dragon Rider Academy. I used to only be able to sense treasure within a few miles as well. Now I have a ten-mile radius, plus I can conjure up images of what the objects look like even if I've never seen them before."

"Are you serious?" Halldor's eyes were wide with astonishment. "I wonder if I'd be able to conjure up images of the people I can sense. That would be really good for reconnaissance."

"We'll ask Tavarian about it later," I said, clapping him on the back. "As for the airship, don't beat yourself up too much about it. We can't be on all the time, and if you hadn't warned us when you did, the damage might have been a lot worse."

"True," Halldor said, but he sounded dubious as he glanced toward the ship. "How long until it's up and running again? I just finished helping Daria go through the inventory—these supplies will last us about a month with our current numbers."

"Well before that," I said confidently. "We just need one of our dragons to make a trip to Warosia."

"Do you need me to do it?"

I considered, then shook my head. "No. You're more valuable here with that talent of yours."

I went indoors to seek out Daria, then got a report from her on the status of our stores. The airship had brought, in addition to food, bedding, tools, kitchen supplies, medical supplies, and a host of other things I hadn't thought of but were sorely needed.

"We definitely need to figure out how we're going to get more money, though," Daria said. "We might be able to scrounge enough together to buy seeds for planting, like we were talking about earlier, but given how hostile the locals are, I wouldn't be surprised if they set our crops on fire."

I sighed, pinching the bridge of my nose to stave off a forming headache. "Ultimately, I think the solution is to find a better place," I said. "The locals are bad enough, but it's only a matter of time before the Zallabarians figure out we're here and attack. We need to find a more remote location before they catch on to us."

Tavarian and I spent the rest of the day discussing plans and strategies with the others before finally retreating to a tower room for the night.

"Ugh," I groaned as I flopped onto the waiting bedroll. "I feel like I haven't slept in a real bed in weeks."

"One week, to be precise," Tavarian teased as he lay down next to me. He wrapped his arms around me, and we both stiffened as his arm brushed against the pouch containing the piece of dragon heart.

"We need to find a place for that, don't we?" I asked quietly. I'd been so distracted all day that I'd completely forgotten about the piece of heart, but now that Tavarian had drawn my attention back to it, I could feel the warped energy emanating from the artifact. With any other artifact I normally would have been tempted to take it out and study it—objectively speaking, it was beautiful, like a huge black diamond that sparkled both in sun and moonlight. But the very nature of its existence repelled me, and I'd had to resist the urge to rip it off my body and chuck it into the ocean on more than one occasion during our flight to Polyba.

"We do," Tavarian said, just as quietly. He slipped his arm from around my waist, then helped me stand. "I wish there was somewhere we could seal it away permanently, but given that we need to take it to the forge to destroy it, the time and effort required would be a waste."

A chill went down my spine at the thought of the quest ahead of us. It was one thing to realize that the gods, after disappearing from our world for millennia, were as alive and well as they'd always been. It was another thing entirely to willingly venture into the domain of Derynnis, the god of death, even if it was to ask him to help me defeat the dragon god. Caor's description of the death god hadn't been encouraging. Apparently, he was the least invested in humanity's welfare, and therefore cared little about saving lives. But then again, if all human life was snuffed out, his steady supply of souls would be cut off, wouldn't it? And considering that he was a god, that had to mean that he hated dragons.

"That's not a mark in his favor," Lessie grumbled, eavesdrop-

ping on my thoughts as she often did. *"Are you sure there isn't another way, Zara?"*

"I wish there was, but there's no time for us to fart around trying to find it," I told her. "Salcombe already has too many pieces as it is. If he manages to get his hands on the one Tavarian left in Elantia, he might become too powerful to stop."

"I wonder what will happen to him once we destroy it?" Lessie asked, and I blinked, surprised at the sudden change in thought. *"Do you think he'll wither away and die without the dragon god's power to boost him up anymore? Or will he go back to being a curmudgeonly old man, living out his days in prison?"*

I repeated the question to Tavarian, but he only shook his head. "There are too many different factors at play to give a definitive answer," he said. "Taking so much of the dragon god's power into his body might very well have harmful effects that could cause him to crumble the moment that influence is removed. But even more concerning is what his state of mind will be like. After all, we don't know if Salcombe sought out the pieces of heart with the intention of resurrecting Zakyiar, or if the dragon god planted the thought in his mind after he got his hands on the first one. Once the dragon god is vanquished, we might very well find that Salcombe's desire to destroy humanity has vanished completely. But killing the god, his entire reason for existing, could make his head spin in."

My stomach twisted at the different scenarios Tavarian presented, and the empathetic side of me, the little girl who'd just been grateful to the man who'd put a roof over her head, found that she hated all of those scenarios. But the rest of me hardened my heart, and I shook my head. "It doesn't matter either way," I said hollowly. Getting my hopes up that Salcombe hadn't intended all this destruction didn't change the fact that he'd still committed heinous crimes against humanity. He had to pay for what he'd done, and I'd see that he did, no matter what it cost me.

THREE

In the end, Tavarian and I hid the piece of heart under a loose flagstone in the tower, near enough that I could get to it easily but far enough away that the effects of its slimy influence were muted. Even so, I had a restless night of sleep, my dreams plagued by darkness. When I woke up the next morning, I felt as if I'd spent the night on a rock slab, tossing and turning, instead of out cold for eight hours on a comfortable mattress.

"Did you sleep any better than I did?" I asked as we trudged downstairs for breakfast.

The shadows carved beneath Tavarian's eyes answered the question before he did. "It's that blasted stone," he muttered. "The dragon god must be trying to attack us in our sleep."

The idea that the dragon god was doing this on purpose was extremely unsettling, but I put that thought aside for later and sat down in the hall with the others for breakfast. This time we had pillows to sit on rather than the harsh stone floor, which already would have made the experience better without the addition of fried potatoes. I felt a little bit guilty that I was sitting on a pillow when not everyone else had one—there were only about thirty pillows, and nearly a hundred people in this room—but everyone seemed to be in high spirits despite the ship's crash-landing, likely because they now had access to soap, toiletries, and bedding.

"You humans are a fussy lot," Lessie remarked. She and the other dragons were flying over the ocean, snatching fish from the waves for their own breakfast after bringing back the catch to feed the riders. *"You need beds, toilets, clothes, cooked food, and fancy drinks. All a dragon needs is fresh meat, clean water, and the open air."*

"Oh, is that all?" I said in mock surprise. "So, you didn't need me to clean out your scale rot the other day?"

I could practically see her tossing her head. *"If I was living in the wild, I would get my mate to do that,"* she said. After a pause, she added, *"But I'm not living in the wild. And I also need you, too, Zara. Don't ever forget it."*

The unexpectedly sappy words brought a smile to my face, banishing the feelings of resentment at the dragon god ruining what was supposed to be a great night of sleep.

"Back atcha," I said, and then turned my attention to business.

After hashing out the day's agenda with the others, it was decided that Rhia and I would go to the other estate to search for the weapon, while Tavarian took a crack at using his diplomatic skills to smooth over relations with the locals. I could tell he wasn't thrilled about the prospect, especially since he'd been looking forward to going to the estate with me, but talking the locals down from their aggressive behavior was more important.

"Do you think he'll be able to get them to back off?" Rhia asked as we flew together on Lessie and Ykos. We still had a few of the magical earpieces left, so we could communicate despite the high winds shrieking around us. "I haven't had the chance to talk much with the natives myself, but despite being Elantian themselves, they seem to have a deep resentment toward us."

"There's probably a story there," I admitted. An arrow whizzed through the air beneath us, missing its mark by a dozen feet, and I pressed my body closer to Lessie's. The locals were still shooting at us, squirreled away in hidden holes in the bushy ground, and we were forced to fly high to avoid their arrows. "This island is pretty inhospitable, and if their ancestors are Elantian, I can't imagine they came here for fun." I wondered if there might have been some bad blood between them and the dragon riders who'd owned the estate here. "But Tavarian has gotten entire nations to change their minds about going to war with diplomacy alone. If he can do that, then surely he can convince a few hundred people to stop shooting us with arrows."

"Maybe," Rhia said dubiously. "But these guys have an unnatural hatred of us. And the only reason Tavarian was able to get Traggar to back off was because of that incident you staged with the Zallabarian ambassador."

The mention of General Trattner reminded me that just a few days ago I'd been sitting in his home at a dinner party, discussing art and artifacts with him. Shortly after that, I'd made a scene, left with another man, and ended up killing that man at his house before absconding with the piece of heart. As far as he was concerned, I was both a murderer and a spy, and he'd let me into not only his home but also within spitting distance of his autocrator.

I shouldn't care about that. It didn't matter what General Trattner thought of me. He was the enemy, after all.

But he had also, for a brief period in time, been my friend.

"A false friendship," Lessie reminded me. *"You did, after all, spike his wine and coerce him into getting himself kicked out of Traggar so Tavarian could convince King Zoltar to back out of the war. Not quite what a true friend would do."*

"You don't have to remind me," I said mulishly. I'd done what I had to, but even though I'd made my living as a thief in the early days and was no stranger to sleight of hand, the deception had bothered me. It made me wonder if I really had the right to judge others who manipulated and deceived people to get what they needed. After all, the ends justified the means, didn't it? And whether or not those ends were morally right all depended on which standpoint you viewed the situation from.

"Yes, we are all the same in the end," Lessie said, nudging me away from the swirling doubt threatening to take over my brain. *"But some of us want to save the world, and the rest of us want to destroy it because we have mommy issues."*

The modern turn of phrase startled a laugh out of me. "Mommy issues? Where did you get that one?"

"It's not as modern as you think," Lessie said smugly. *"Remember, I've been listening to other people's conversations for hundreds of yea—"*

A *plink* distracted us as an arrow struck Lessie's scales. I cringed as she roared loud enough to make my ears vibrate, and instinctively hunkered down, away from the sound. Rage blazed through our bond, and, ignoring my shouts completely, both dragons dove toward the bushes.

"No!" I cried as they spewed fire at the enemy. Two scrawny boys jumped out of a hole as the brush caught fire. My heart leapt into my throat as I watched them race away, their legs pumping as hard as they could to outrun the spreading blaze. There were many dry bushes clumped close together, and I watched with dismay as the fire spread across the entire hillside, forcing birds and rabbits to flee the area.

"STOP!" I infused my voice with as much willpower as I could muster, and Lessie came to a halt in midair, the magic in our bond compelling her. Ykos drew up beside her, and Rhia and I glared at our respective dragons. A long moment passed as we hovered there, trying to get a handle on our emotions again.

"I don't ever want to have to use our bond to force you to comply," I finally said, my jaw clenching so hard that the lower half of my face ached. *"Do you understand?"*

"I wasn't going to kill them," Lessie said sourly. *"I just wanted to give them a healthy dose of fear. Maybe now they'll think twice about shooting at us again."*

I threw up my hands in the air. *"And maybe now instead of shooting at dragons flying in the sky, they'll sneak up to our camp and set the whole damn thing on fire! They probably know that killing the riders will also kill the dragons, Lessie. And since you guys keep stealing their livestock, they're understandably resentful!"*

"It's not my fault the other dragons are imbeciles!" Lessie

snapped back. *"I didn't steal any livestock, because I was in Zallabar, rescuing your hide!"*

I sucked in a deep breath, trying for patience. *"I know,"* I said, gentling my voice. *"And I appreciate that. But Tavarian is out there right now trying to reason with the locals. Going after their children isn't going to help. The arrows they're shooting at us are harmless as long as we stay up in the sky, and you know it."*

"Fine." Lessie let out a long sigh, and twin plumes of smoke jetted out of her nostrils. *"I will endeavor to be nicer to the murderous humans."*

I patted the side of her neck. *"That's the spirit."*

We continued on, reaching the estate a few minutes later. "Do you sense anything?" Rhia asked as we hovered over the property. It was twice as large as the first one, but in even worse repair, with hardly any roofing left intact and walls that were so decrepit they might as well have been lattices. To my relief, it didn't look like anyone occupied it—there were no signs that anyone lived here and, judging by the lack of arrows flying through the air, no one waiting to ambush us.

Clearing my head, I called on my treasure sense and focused on the area. "I don't sense anything from up here," I told her after a moment, "but we should go down and investigate, just in case. There might be some clues that can tell us more."

We landed in the courtyard, and I let out a sigh of relief as my feet touched solid ground. Normally, I was happiest in the sky, but after that encounter, I wanted to put a little space between me and Lessie until we'd both cooled down a bit more.

I knew it was bound to happen eventually, but the argument had left me feeling more than a little unsettled.

"All right," I said, putting it out of my mind and focusing my treasure sense again. "Let's comb this place thoroughly."

We spent an hour searching the ruins for any sign of a weapon. I knew I wasn't going to actually find the weapon itself here—if my treasure sense hadn't picked it up from the sky, it certainly wasn't going to do better here—but we hoped to find something that could at least tell us what kind of weapon we were looking for, maybe even a secret passage with diaries or clues the locals hadn't found. But the estate had been picked clean, not even a scrap of pottery left behind.

"I had wondered if maybe the weapon could have been something that your treasure sense wouldn't pick up on," Rhia said as we sat on the edge of a crumbling wall, looking out at the arid landscape. "Like maybe a vat of special poison hidden away somewhere, or a recipe or instructions to build something formidable. But there's nothing here, is there?"

"No." I twirled a corroded silver spoon in my hand that I'd found buried in the dirt—trampled, more likely—and considered the birds wheeling over the forest a few miles away. If we had a few bows, we could hunt them.

"*Perhaps a slingshot?*" Lessie said. "*That girl, Aria, was surprisingly effective with the one she used on you.*"

I gritted my teeth as that encounter reared up in my mind, as fresh as though it had happened yesterday. I'd been flying on Lessie—our first attempt together—when Aria, Jallis's jealous ex-girlfriend, had hit me with a projectile using her slingshot. Unprepared, and with no stirrups to keep me on Lessie's back, I'd tumbled out of the sky and nearly to my death.

That shot had only been a few hundred feet in the air, much

higher than I thought one could shoot with a slingshot. But it was certainly enough to take down birds, so long as one could be sneaky and quiet.

"Hey, Rhia—" I looked over at her, about to share my suggestion, but the words died in my throat at the tear tracks on her face. "What's wrong?"

"I've brought us here for nothing," she said in a tortured voice. Her lower lip trembled as she tried to swipe the tears from her face, but more kept coming. "If the weapon isn't here, then all this trouble we've gone through has been wasted."

"Don't be silly. Sure, we've had some setbacks, but the weapon could still be on this island, and we haven't lost any li—"

"It's not just that!" she wailed, and suddenly I remembered that Rhia was only nineteen, barely an adult. She always presented such a strong and capable front, taking on problems without a word of complaint, I forgot that, in actuality, she was very inexperienced. "It's everything—the shock of losing the war, being separated from my family, watching my comrades get cut down and blasted to pieces by the enemy! I have nightmares, Zara, that I'll return home to Elantia one day and find only my mother's grave waiting for me. Last night I dreamed that I walked into my home and she was sitting by the hearth, a skeleton wearing her best day dress. She stood up to give me a hug, and her bones fell apart."

The last part came out as a half-sob, half-shriek that broke my heart into a million pieces. Swallowing against the sudden lump in my throat, I wrapped my arms around her and hugged her tight. The sobs grew louder as she buried her face in my chest, and I held on as she let out all the grief that had clearly been festering in her heart for weeks.

"I-I'm sorry," she hiccuped, pulling back to wipe at her ruddy face. "I didn't mean to lose it like that. It's just—"

"You don't have to explain." I squeezed her hand and gave her a gentle smile. "If I had family back home in Elantia, I would be worried sick about them too. I worry about Carina and the orphans every day, but I know that's not the same as blood relatives." I'd come to consider Carina and the orphans my family, but I knew the love I felt for them had nothing on the bond I'd seen between parents and their children. "To be honest, the horrors I've seen have given me nightmares too." I still sometimes dreamt of that horrid battlefield Tavarian had walked through, littered with dead soldiers from both sides, the giant bodies of dragons lying broken and still in pools of blood. "I think having the piece of heart nearby is making things worse, so the sooner I leave for the forge, the better."

"You mean the sooner we leave." I opened my mouth to argue, but Rhia cut me off with a dry look. "There's no way you're going on a quest to speak with an ancient death god and leaving me behind. I've missed out on all sorts of adventures since the two of us were sent to different camps, and Ykos and I aren't missing out on this one for the world."

I laughed. "You do realize we could all die horribly, right?"

Rhia spread her arms wide, as if to indicate the inhospitable land around us. "And we could die horribly on this island, too. If I'm going to die, I at least want it to be a glorious end. Wouldn't you agree?"

I'd never been one for dying in glorious endings—in fact, I'd much prefer to be lying in a comfy bed or curled up with Lessie when I finally passed—but I wasn't going to rain on Rhia's parade when she was finally looking in better spirits.

"All right," I said, clapping her on the back. "One horrible death, coming right up."

She giggled, and even though there might have been a little bit of hysteria in the sound, I'd take it over the crying. Finished at the estate, we mounted up and headed back to base. The return flight was uneventful, with not a single arrow shot from the sky, and I surmised the two boys we'd scared had spread the word.

"I might not agree with what you did, but I admit this is much more pleasant," I said to Lessie.

"Of course it is," she said, a smirk in her voice. But then she added, *"I do see your point, though, and I will tell the other dragons to make efforts not to exacerbate relations with the natives."*

"That would be much appreciated."

"Hey," Rhia said. "Isn't that Tavarian and Halldor on the ground?"

I looked over the side of Lessie's neck toward where Rhia pointed. Sure enough, Tavarian and Halldor stood there, talking to four very irate-looking men. They were about half a mile away from the settlement they'd gone to visit, and the men very much looked like they'd like to bolt in that direction if not for Halldor's dragon blocking their way.

"Let me check it out while you keep watch," I said to Rhia.

By unspoken agreement, Lessie swooped down toward the group of men. The strangers looked like they were about to wet themselves as Lessie came near, but I merely jumped off her back and landed in a crouch next to Tavarian, and the men let out a sigh of relief as she passed by them.

"Zara!" Tavarian broke off the discussion as he turned toward me, looking mildly surprised. "I take it you and Rhia have finished at the estate. Did you find anything?"

I shook my head. "The estate has been completely cleared out. We'll have to try the settlements next. Any luck with the natives? It would help if they were on board with the search."

"Not precisely," Tavarian said with a sigh. "We went to the closest village, but the doors on all the homes were barred, and no one would speak to us or answer us. That said," he added, clapping Halldor on the shoulder, "Captain Halldor's talent helped us locate these four men, who were hiding in an underground cellar." He pointed to two wooden doors I hadn't spotted from the sky, partially hidden by a clump of bushes. "We are trying to come to an understanding."

"What is there to understand?" one of the men spat. He was bald and wiry, with a thick mustache and brows that I imagined made him look intimidating even when he wasn't angry. "You are trespassing on our land, and you need to leave!"

"And we've already explained that we don't intend to stay!" Halldor said hotly, and I winced. Perhaps he hadn't been the best choice to bring along to a diplomatic discussion, but he'd wanted to help after what had happened that morning. "We're just here to look for an item that the dragon riders who lived here might have left behind. Believe me, we intend to leave this forsaken place as soon as possible."

"What Halldor means to say," Tavarian said in a pleasant

voice after giving him a warning look, "is that the sooner we can find this item we are looking for, the faster we can be on our way. It would help us tremendously if we could understand what the cause of all this resentment toward us is, and if there is anything we can do to fix it. We do not wish to cause trouble, and we certainly do not wish to fight with you or disrupt your way of life."

"Hmph." The men did not look entirely convinced, but one sporting several facial piercings and a geometric pattern shaved into his close-cropped scalp spoke up. "Dragon rider memories may not be long, but the Ariban family never forgets. Our ancestors were brought here by you dragon riders to help work the land and the estates here hundreds of years ago. The elders say that even then the rich treated us like mud, but at least we had plenty of work and food."

"At least until the drought," the bald man grunted. "That was fifty years ago, and it continues to plague the island. The riders must have done something to anger the gods, and instead of fixing it, they abandoned this island and left us to starve."

"We have only barely managed to carve out a living here, only now for you to return and steal our precious resources!" one of the other men cried, and then all four began shouting at once. They might have even worked themselves up into a frenzy, but Kiethara, Halldor's dragon, let out an ear-splitting roar that shook the ground and silenced everyone instantly.

"I am sorry that your people have suffered so," Tavarian said in the deafening silence. "You are Elantian citizens, and you should not have been left stranded in this unforgiving climate. If our country were still at peace, I would have my airship bring you back to the mainland, and get you settled somewhere with good farmland and plenty of water, paid for by the family that abandoned you here. Unfortunately, our country has been taken by the Zallabarians. The only reason we are here is because we are searching for a weapon that was rumored to have been left behind here, something that may help us take back our country."

"Zallabarians?" For the first time, the men looked worried. "We don't know anything about them, but they must be strong to have taken the entire country. How long has this war been going on?"

"Just a few weeks," Tavarian said grimly.

The men goggled. "Only a few weeks? And the country is already lost?"

"Not completely lost," Halldor said irritably. "They tried to capture our dragons to use for themselves, but we managed to rescue them. That's why they're all here on the island with us. We just escaped from Zallabarian territory."

"It's only a matter of time before the Zallabarians turn their attention to this island," I told them. "Normally, they wouldn't have much interest in a place like this, but they will be very interested if the dragons are still here. Please, help us find this weapon so we can leave."

"We don't know about any weapon!" the bald man snapped. "The Porcillas family did most of the looting in that other estate you mentioned—we barely got anything! You'll have to speak to them if you want to find this weapon, but I doubt they have anything or they would have used it to wipe out the other families on the island already. They are very nasty, vindictive people."

"And speaking of the Porcillas family, you had better watch out," the man with the piercing warned. "I heard they lost two men last night in that ambush against you, and they will not be satisfied until they are paid in blood."

Tavarian sighed. "I was afraid you might say that."

"What does that mean?" Halldor demanded. "That they won't be satisfied until they kill two of us? But they attacked us first, not the other way around!"

"We Polybans practice blood vengeance," the third man, bulkier than the others, said proudly. "So yes, the Porcillas family will continue to attack until they claim two lives for the lives they lost. They cannot be bought off, and their clan is nearly two-thousand members strong."

"Shit," I muttered, scraping a hand through my hair. Two thousand? It was a good thing Halldor could sense people and that our dragons had such good hearing, because they could massacre us overnight otherwise. "How many families are on the island?"

"There are six of us total," Baldy said. "The Porcillas family is the largest, but our clan is fairly large as well. And with so many people on the island, it is a battle every day to feed all of us. This island cannot afford to support you and your dragons as well, so the other clans will be coming after you too. It is only a matter of time."

"We will do our best to consume as few resources as possible," Tavarian promised, "and we will be leaving as soon as we can. In fact, our airship was bringing back supplies so we wouldn't have to rely on the land, and it would have gone out to bring back more if the Porcillases hadn't damaged it. Once we get it fixed, we will bring back supplies for your clan in return for your chief's support."

The bald man grunted, but the men's eyes gleamed. Tavarian had finally piqued their interest. "We cannot make any promises," he said. "But we will speak to our chief and let him know of your offer."

"Thank you," Tavarian said. "That's all I ask."

The disgruntled men finally left, skirting nervously around Halldor's dragon while they cast suspicious glances over their shoulders at us.

"I know we are running low on funds," Rhia said, "but is there any chance we might be able to hire some of the locals to cook for us? If we traded goods for labor, I'm sure they would be more than happy, especially considering how scarce food is around here."

"That would be a good idea, Rhia, if the natives weren't so hostile," Tavarian said. "As it is, we could not trust anyone we hire not to poison our food or try to kill us in our sleep."

"They already tried to poison us with those sheep," Halldor pointed out. "No way would I trust any of them in our camp."

"Right." Rhia's cheeks colored as Halldor's dragon let out a low growl. Rhia had already forgotten the incident, and as it was Halldor's dragon, that only made it more embarrassing.

"Hey." Noticing Rhia's discomfort, Halldor moved closer and gave her a reassuring pat on the shoulder. "I didn't take any offense, so don't sweat it. I know how overwhelmed you've been trying to run things around here, and you're doing a great job."

"You really think so?" Rhia's blush deepened with an

entirely different kind of embarrassment, and I had to hold back a smirk.

"Absolutely." Grinning, Halldor gave her a one-armed hug, then steered her back to Ykos, who waited nearby with Lessie. "Now, let's get back to base so we can figure out where to go from here."

We mounted up, then returned to camp and held another meeting with Jallis. The four of us made a list of all the problems that still needed to be solved: digging new latrines, finding a team of cooks, procuring more funds, dealing with the Porcillas's threat, and finding the weapon. Jallis promised to find a volunteer to leave for Warosia as soon as possible, and he and Rhia left to go check in with the others.

"We'll need to hold a council meeting soon," Tavarian said. "In addition to these issues, we also need to discuss our trip to the forge, and where to go next. Given that we have no other options, the others may have to stay here while we are gone, but if we cannot come to an agreement with the locals, that may be too dangerous."

"I know." I massaged my aching temples. There was so much to do, so many threats to deal with—fighting in the war and dealing with Salcombe was easier than this in some ways, as at least I only had to focus on one objective, and I was only responsible for Lessie and myself. Now I was responsible for over one hundred riders and dragons, the last remnants of Elantia's legacy. No way in hell was I going to let them get wiped out on my watch, especially not by a few thousand locals with only arrows and spears.

"Is it bad that I'm looking forward to our trip to the forge?" I said to Tavarian, only half-joking.

He smirked. "Better than quaking in your boots with fear, don't you think?"

True. The latter was probably a healthier response. But then again, nobody went on dangerous quests or took on dragon gods without having a little crazy in them. And I had a feeling I would need a whole lot more crazy if we were going to get through this in one piece.

FOUR

"You got this?" Jallis asked as I tied the rope onto the pommel of Lessie's saddle.

I tested the rope, which was attached to my end of a very large net, and nodded. "It should hold." Or at least that's what I figured. After all, Ullion had gone out with another dragon rider to do this the day before. How hard could it be?

Lessie tossed her head. *"I can't believe we're doing this,"* she grumbled. *"We are dragons, not fishermen!"*

"Right now, we're whatever the group needs us to be," I reminded her. *"And with the airship down for repairs, we have to keep catching fish to supplement our rations."*

I gave Jallis the thumbs up, and after counting to three, the four of us took flight. For a minute, I was worried Lessie wouldn't be able to fly in sync with Kadryn, who was still larger than her despite her alarmingly frequent growth spurts. But though she had to beat her wings a little harder than him, she kept pace.

"I'm so proud of you," I told her. "You've come such a long way."

Lessie didn't say anything, but I could feel her heart swell with pride through the bond. We seemed to have smoothed things over since our fight two days ago—she'd admitted she was wrong, and I apologized for being overly harsh. Sometimes it was hard to remember that Lessie was barely a year old, and that she hadn't been disobeying me out of spite. Despite her moments of wisdom and her advanced vocabulary, she was still a child in many ways, and not always able to see the bigger picture.

"Isn't that why I have you around?" she teased. *"So you can be the brains, and I can be the brawn?"*

"I'd like to think I bring a fair bit of brawn to the table," I said with a grin.

"Maybe, but I'd like to see you beat me in an arm-wrestling match."

"You ready?" Jallis asked through the earpiece, breaking up the banter. "Kadryn says this is a good spot."

"Yep. Let's go."

Lessie and Kadryn lined up the net so the two sides were level, then dove toward the water together. They flew as low as they could, their bellies skimming the waves, and I laughed, holding up my hands to shield myself as the salty sea spray spattered my clothing and hair. A few seconds later, the two dragons brought up the net, and Jallis and I cheered at the sight of several hundred fish inside, their scales flashing as they tried to wriggle free.

Unfortunately, Lessie shot up a little too fast, and the net slid too far back. "Dammit!" Jallis swore as the fish waterfalled back into the ocean.

"Sorry," Lessie said sheepishly. *I got a little too excited to get them back to the base.*

It took three tries, but eventually we managed to catch the fish and keep the net steady as we carried it back to the coast. As we landed in the courtyard to hand over the catch to the four riders who were unwillingly drafted to assist with prepping and cooking the fish—we all rotated shifts daily, hence why Jallis and I were out here—something glimmered high in the sky. Turning around fully, I slipped on my goggles and zoomed in to get a better look.

"*Newcomers!*" Lessie cried as I locked on to two enormous dragons flying through the sky. The riders on their backs appeared to be elderly, with lined faces and white hair.

"They must be escaping from the mainland," Jallis said, sounding worried. "How did they find us?"

That's a damn good question, I thought as the riders landed. Their dragons were too large to fit in the courtyard with both Kadryn, Lessie, and the catch, so they soared past us to the field where the other dragons were headed.

Leaving the fish to the others, I hopped onto Lessie, unhooked the net, and took off to where the newcomers were. To my surprise, Halldor was already there, talking to the riders as if he knew them.

"Commandant," he greeted me as I dismounted. "This is Sirion and Nimor, of House Callias."

"Pleasure to meet you," I said to them, but my attention was still on the captain. "Did you know they were coming?"

"Kiethara got a message from Sirion's dragon while you were out." He pointed to the dragon on the left, his hide a charcoal gray woven through with glimmering silver. "Apparently he has a longer telepathic range than most dragons, which was how he was able to find the island."

"I see." I wished Rhia was here to interrogate them. My instinct was to trust them, but given our precarious position and the fact that at least one dragon rider had already defected to the Zallabarians' side, we couldn't risk that these two hadn't been turned.

"You don't seem very happy to see us," Nimor commented with a frown. He was a little hardier-looking than Sirion, with keen blue eyes and a frank stare. "I thought you would be pleased to know there are more dragons alive."

"I'm sorry," I said, feeling a little guilty about my cold welcome. After all, these guys had probably gone through hell recently, just like the rest of us, and flying long distances couldn't be easy on them anymore. "Please, come and rest inside. You can fill us in on your story over lunch."

I asked Halldor to fetch Rhia and Tavarian, then led the two riders to a private room off the main hall.

Rhia and Tavarian joined us shortly, bringing bread and cheese from the rations as well as a pitcher of water. "Sorry about the meager fare," I said as they tore into the food. "It's after breakfast and the fish we caught for lunch isn't going to be ready for a while."

"Oh no, this is wonderful," Sirion said. "We've had nothing to eat but meat and berries for the past few days, so this is a nice change of pace."

I took a minute to introduce the rest of the people in the room, then prompted the two riders to tell us their story. "What news do you have from the mainland?" I asked.

"It is a terrible time for dragon riders," Nimor said sadly. "The Zallabarians are destroying all living dragons they encounter and confiscating any dragon eggs they can find. We thought we would be safe since we both live in remote country estates, well hidden away, but the enemy has managed to rally even the country folk to their sides. They have been ratting out our locations, forcing us to flee so they can loot our estates and steal our land. The only reason Sirion and I escaped is because our servants warned us what was coming."

"That's terrible," Rhia said, her voice full of sympathy. Her lack of reaction told me that the men were telling the truth, and I relaxed a little even as my heart ached for their plight.

"Terrible doesn't even begin to cover it," Sirion said. While his partner was sad, his dark eyes blazed with pent-up rage. "If I were a young man and my dragon were stronger, I would have stayed and fought with everything I had. They're not just killing our dragons, they're also taking away our children!"

"Dragon rider children?" I frowned, remembering the children Rhia had brought with her when we met up in Ruisin. I exchanged a worried glance with Tavarian.

"Are they only taking dragon rider children?" Tavarian asked them. "Or commoners as well?"

"Just dragon rider children, and only boys," Nimor said with a puzzled frown. "I imagine that's because there are no women in the Zallabarian army. The only thing we can think of is that they're planning to brainwash our children and the newly hatched dragons into fighting for them."

"I wonder why the autocrator is putting so much time and effort into this," Jallis said with a frown. "After all, he's already proven that he doesn't need dragons to win wars. Much as it pains me to say it, it would be easier to kill them all."

"I have met Reichstein on two occasions, back when he was still just a general," Tavarian said, his tone turning sour with distaste. "The man is ruthless and pragmatic, but he is also quite forward-thinking. My guess is that he sees a military use for the dragons that we have not thought of, possibly a pairing of dragon riders and technology."

"What, you mean like mounting guns on the backs of dragons?" The very idea sent a chill through my bones. "Why would that be better than just using airships?"

"Dragons can execute all kinds of maneuvers in the air that ships can't," Jallis pointed out reluctantly. "If we'd had guns mounted on the backs of our dragons, the war might have gone differently."

The older dragons looked appalled at the idea, so I quickly changed the subject. "Did you have any other news for us?"

Nimor opened the flap of the brown leather satchel slung around his shoulder and removed a large oval object wrapped in thick cloth. "No, but we did manage to save these eggs on our way out." Everyone in the room sucked in sharp breaths as he laid out three dragon eggs on the floor. They shimmered like jewels in the shaft of light coming through the window, and my breath caught as I remembered the first time I'd laid eyes on Lessie's egg. I'd barely realized what I'd been holding when she decided to hatch after lying dormant for hundreds of years, and that moment had changed my life forever.

Now, here were three shining opportunities for other lives to be changed. So long as the Zallabarians didn't find us here first.

"Please, Commandant," Sirion implored. "You must send a contingent back to Elantia and rescue the remaining dragon eggs. If we can also rescue the male children, so much the better, but it is absolutely imperative that we seize the rest of the eggs while there is still a chance."

I froze, torn between the desire to help and the instinct to stay as far away from the enemy as possible. "Do you have any idea which families have yet to be hit?" Tavarian asked.

"I'm afraid not," Nimor said. "But we can tell you which ones have already been targeted, which may help narrow things down."

We took down the list from the two riders, then called an emergency council meeting in the great hall. In addition to the men and women I'd come to depend on—Ullion, Kade, Daria, Rhia, Jallis, and Halldor—there were also ten others, all high-ranking officers of varying ages and temperaments. Jallis knew them all far better than I did after being stuck with them in that Zallabarian prison mine, but after a few days here I was already learning their names.

As expected, Sirion and Nimor's news caused an uproar amongst the council members. "I have two little brothers back home!" Byron, a hot-headed lieutenant with unruly blond hair, shouted as he jumped to his feet. "We need to go back to Elantia right away and rescue the remaining children."

"My mother has two eggs hidden on our property," Daria said, her face pale. "Do you think they've taken them already?"

"We will mount a rescue mission to retrieve as many eggs and children as we can," Tavarian said sternly. Somehow, he managed to pitch his voice above the clamor without raising it, and the din died down a bit. "But no one is running off half-cocked to do this by themselves. We will form a plan and execute it. Understood?"

Mutterings of "yes" rippled through the room, while others were more enthusiastic. "We should try to take back whatever gold and valuables we can as well," one of the older officers said eagerly. "We need all we can if we're going to establish a proper base and fight back."

"I do have something in mind regarding that," I said. "If we plan this right, there's no reason we can't kill three birds with one stone."

We started off our agenda by making a list of all known dragon children and eggs at risk, as well as who would be in charge of rescuing them. Since they were fairly spread out around the country, we decided it would be best to send teams of three to each of Elantia's ten prefectures—thirty riders total—and an additional ten to ferret out any gold and treasure we could take back with us.

"Is it worth it to attempt a rescue at Zuar City?" one of the officers argued. "We all know the city is firmly under Zallabarian control and will be heavily guarded."

"They will have already evicted everyone from Dragon's Table by now, and taken over the residences themselves," Tavarian said grimly. "Zara and I can attempt a flyover, since I have my cloaking spell, to see if there are any dragons in the area, but I doubt we will be able to get anywhere."

I met Rhia's eyes from across the room and felt a squirm of guilt as she blinked back tears. I knew she was thinking of her mother, whom she'd been forced to leave behind. By the time she'd reached Zuar City, sent to warn them of the attack, they had already been hit and she'd barely escaped with her life. "We'll let you know if we find anything," I said, and she nodded tersely. It was the best I could do.

"So where are we taking the gold from?" Kade asked, his eyes gleaming. I could tell the prospect of a treasure hunt excited him, even if we were risking our lives to do it. "Are we going to break into the estates the Zallabarians have taken over? It's little more than what they deserve, and if they can't pay their troops, so much the better."

"That would be extremely dangerous," Tavarian said. "We don't have the necessary intelligence, and even if we did, those estates are likely well-armed."

"What about the floating islands?" Daria asked. "The Zallabarians haven't occupied Elantia for very long. It's likely they've left them untouched."

Tavarian and I exchanged startled glances. "That's...an excellent idea," he said. "I'm not sure why I didn't think of it myself."

Daria grinned. "You two don't have to think of everything," she said. "We're a team, and the rest of us can contribute too."

"You're absolutely right." I smiled as Daria's words settled around my shoulders like a warm blanket. Tavarian and I didn't have to think of everything on our own. The men and women we'd surrounded ourselves with were smart and capable, more so than me in many ways. I might have been their reluctant leader, but there was no reason I couldn't lean on them for support and guidance when needed.

The cooking volunteers announced that the fish was ready, so we had lunch brought into the council room while we continued to hash out the details of our rescue operation. I was halfway through my plate when Halldor suddenly jumped up from his seat and rushed to the window.

"There's a ship approaching!" he shouted. "With roughly four hundred passengers aboard!"

"Four hundred?" I nearly shrieked. "What flag are they flying?"

"They're running one up the mast right now," Halldor said. "It's...Elantian."

"Damn." We raced out of the room collectively, and ten of us armored up and winged our way to the rocky shoreline to meet them. The settlement was located only a mile from there, and we knew that the locals would be waiting, ready to attack the newcomers and steal any resources they'd brought.

Sure enough, there were several hundred locals waiting by the shore, armed with spears and bows and wooden swords. "No fire!" I shouted to the others as we dove toward them.

Thankfully, the other dragons obeyed, keeping their flames firmly banked in their bellies. We swooped over the crowd, low enough for the dragons to knock back the villagers with the gusts of wind from their great beating wings, but high enough that they couldn't easily hurt us. A few stray arrows bounced off my dragon rider armor, and two of the riders got nicked, but after seeing how their projectiles bounced harmlessly off dragon hide, the villagers turned tail and ran for the hills.

"Good job," I told Lessie as I patted her neck. *"Now let's go see who these people are."*

Lessie flew over to the ship. Despite the flag, it seemed to be of Warosian make. None of the men and women on board showed any fear when we landed on deck, and when Tavarian and I dismounted, a man stepped forward to greet us. He, like everyone else on board, wore a tattered gray shirt and trousers, but his air of command told me he was in charge.

"Good afternoon," he said in an upper-crust Elantian accent. "I am Captain Ragorin, and these are my fellow soldiers. We recently heard that the dragons and their riders were liberated in a daring rescue, and so we staged an escape of our own from the POW camp where we were held and came to find you. Are you the ones who executed the rescue mission?"

"We are," I said. "I'm Zara Kenrook, and this is Lord Varrick Tavarian. Are you seeking refuge with us?"

"We are," he confirmed. "We don't have anywhere else to go."

I sighed. "There are people on the island, Elantians who were abandoned there a long time ago, who are extremely hostile to outsiders due to a lack of natural resources on the island. They are going to be furious if we bring you ashore."

"Well, you're going to have to." A man wearing a tri-cornered hat stepped forward. The brass pommel of his sword stuck out from behind his long blue coat, and his clothes looked much finer than the rags the soldiers wore. "I'm Captain Longforth, and this is my ship. I agreed to help these men because they couldn't stay where they were, but I can't keep them aboard my ship indefinitely. They're going to have to get off here whether you like it or not."

"We weren't planning on turning them away, Captain," Tavarian assured him. "We just want the men to understand what they're walking into."

The captain brought the ship to shore, and the soldiers disembarked via rope ladder, dropping into the waves and swimming ashore. Tavarian and I thanked the captain for his assistance, then flew back to the base, helping the other riders escort the soldiers and protect them from any locals still thinking about striking out.

"Great," Daria grumbled under her breath as we headed back in. "Just when I thought we had enough bedding and supplies, this happens. Where are these guys going to sleep?"

"We're happy to camp out in the main hall at night," the captain said from behind us. "As for food, we all know how to hunt and live off the land."

"Hunting is scarce here, and the locals see us as trespassing no matter where we go," I warned him. "Your men will need to be prepared for confrontations, and you cannot, under any circumstances, steal the livestock or the crops. These men and women may not like us, but they're still Elantians. We have no right to steal from them."

"Understood," Ragorin said, and he sounded like he meant it.

We brought the soldiers into the main hall and told the rest of the riders who they were and where they came from. Many of them were dismayed at the addition of so many mouths to feed, but others recognized them as potential manpower for the fight ahead. As I gazed at the sea of people, another headache started to brew behind my forehead. Just when I thought we'd handled the rations, even if temporarily, we'd increased our numbers to five times what we started with.

"We're going to have to go fishing five times a day," Lessie said gloomily, and I might have laughed if I didn't half think it was true myself.

Thankfully, the dragon riders didn't grumble about the newcomers very long. Soon enough, they were helping the others figure out how to settle in, giving the bulk of the fish we'd caught to the men and breaking out more rations. "We were in the middle of a council meeting when you arrived," I told Ragorin. "As the leader of your men, you should join us."

"Of course." He quickened his step to keep pace with me and Tavarian as we headed back to the council chamber. "I'm sure I'll be able to be of some help."

We all sat down again, and with Rhia in the room to vet every word, Captain Ragorin told about the escape. Inspired by the dragon riders' escape, they'd managed to break out of the prisoner camp in the middle of the night and had fought their way through to the Warosian border.

"The Warosians wouldn't let us stay, of course," Ragorin said, "but they did let us pass through, and with the help of Captain Longforth, we managed to make it here. At first, we weren't sure where to go, but by the third day of our escape, your location had become common knowledge."

The blood drained from every face in the room. "The Zallabarians know we're here?"

"I would assume so, since the Warosians do. In every town

we scouted for intelligence, people were talking about rumors of a dragon rider base in Polyba. Apparently, some sailors saw you guys land here, and they helpfully decided to spread the news."

"Damn." Tavarian rubbed his jaw. "We were hoping to remain undetected a little longer. Even with five hundred men, we will be hard-pressed to defend the island if the Zallabarians decide to mount an assault."

"Then we will need to move as soon as possible," Ragorin said. " I'm wondering why you haven't already."

We explained about the airship accident, as well as the secret weapon we were looking for.

"A weapon that could devastate the Zallabarians, eh?" Ragorin said as he scratched at his unruly beard. He likely hadn't been given the opportunity to shave or trim it since being captured. Nearly all the men with him sported unkempt beards and overgrown hair, against regulation. "Well, that's certainly worth sticking around for, but we'll have to search for it double-time. In the meantime, my men and I are more than happy to help with anything you need. There are several cooks amongst us, as well as mechanics who can help repair the damaged airship."

"Real mechanics would help tremendously," Tavarian said, brightening for the first time since this conversation had started. "We might be able to shave a week off the repairs if we have experienced hands working on it."

I certainly hope so, I thought. There was no way the dragons could carry all five hundred men across an entire ocean, and if that airship wasn't ready to go by the time the Zallabarians turned their attention our way, we were toast.

FIVE

I spent the rest of the day out with Jallis, catching hundreds of fish to bring back for our exponentially larger army, as well as preparing defenses should the Zallabarians attack our base before we were ready to leave. Tavarian, Rhia, and I would likely have to start our quest for the forge before the airship was repaired, and I wanted to make sure the base was as well defended and prepared as possible before we left.

By the time my head hit the pillow that night, my eyelids slammed shut and I fell asleep. But the deep, dreamless sleep I hoped for did not come, and I found myself racing through the darkness, trying to outrun the insidious voice whispering in my ear.

Give it up, Zara, it cooed, wrapping around me like black silk on naked skin. *This burden you carry is so heavy. Surely you can put it down for a little while.*

It was heavy, I realized, glancing down at my arms. At first, I thought I was holding a swaddled baby, but nestled in the cloth was the piece of heart, a black diamond that glittered even in the absence of all light. It seemed to glow from within, an eerie red light that was as mesmerizing as it was repulsive. I wanted to hold it close. I wanted to throw it far, far away.

I just needed a break from all of this.

"No!" I shouted, trying to snap myself out of the funk. But a great clawed hand appeared before me, twice as large as my entire body. Talons the length of my arm extended toward me, toward the diamond, and I reached for my dragon blade only to find it wasn't there...

"Are you looking for this?"

A familiar voice pierced the darkness, and the dragon god roared as a shaft of light struck the space between us. I gasped at the sight of my dragon blade standing right there, sticking out of the ground like a double-ended spear. I lunged for the weapon, and it came into my hand almost before I touched it, spinning and bending to my will as it always had.

"Get back!" I cried, slashing at the dragon god's hand. White fire rippled along the wound, and the dragon roared again. Anger and pain reverberated through my skull as the white fire spread, engulfing everything until there was nothing but light...until there was nothing at all.

"Not quite nothing." I spun around to see Caor standing behind me. The messenger god regarded me from those lapis lazuli eyes with a mildly amused expression, dressed in nothing but his usual kilt, torque, and winged sandals. I must have dropped the piece of heart when I'd reached for my blade, as it hovered above his outstretched hand, suspended by a pulse of golden light. "I believe this belongs to you," he prompted, holding it out to me.

I gave him a wry smile as I stepped forward. "I think the dragon god would disagree."

Caor frowned, his wings fluttering with agitation. "Regardless of who it belongs to, you must get rid of it, Zara. Why have you not already left for the Forge of Derynnis? You could have been halfway there by now."

"Because I have a responsibility to my people," I said, snatching the piece of heart from him. The black diamond was frigid to the touch despite the fire burning within, and I quickly wrapped it up in the cloth I'd dropped to the ground before I got frostbite or something. "If I'm going to abandon them on a weeks-long quest that I might die trying to complete, I want them to be prepared first. I didn't go through all the trouble of rescuing them only to let them die the moment I turn my back."

"Fair point." Caor let out a theatrical sigh. "You humans really are far too fragile, but then again we made you that way, so I suppose there's no one to blame but ourselves." He gave an equally theatrical shrug that made me want to strangle him. "I have half a mind to snap my fingers and send you straight to the forge, except that Derynnis would toss you out on your arse before you could open your mouth. He does not believe in shortcuts. If you wish to speak with him, you must reach the island without divine intervention."

"Wonderful," I grumbled. I'd been hoping Caor might be

able to give me a little help. When I'd retrieved the piece of heart from Baron Fersel in Barkheim, Caor had used his godly influence to help me get past the guards and escape with my life. But if I was to do this without any "divine intervention," as he pointed out, that meant I could count on no such luck from him.

"Did you come to tell me anything useful?" I asked. "Or just to save me from my nightmare?"

"Mostly just to nudge you," he admitted. "Though I do sympathize with your plight. A good night of sleep is essential if one is to go adventuring, or so I'm told. Gods don't need sleep. Oh!" He snapped his fingers, as if remembering something. "You might like to know that Salcombe was taken into custody after you murdered Baron Fersel. As your alleged husband, the Zallabarians naturally think he was in league with you."

It was my turn to shrug. "Well, if I hadn't gotten to the baron first, Salcombe definitely would have killed him to get the piece of heart." With the dragon god's power to aid him, he likely would have ripped through the entire staff like they were a house of paper dolls. I'd left most of them alive, and I wouldn't have killed any of them at all if Fersel hadn't decided I needed to be permanently silenced to protect his secret.

"Yes, that was a nasty business," Caor said. "I would have thought Fersel would side with you, but he tried to kill you, proof that no matter how many millennia pass, humans remain as unpredictable as ever." He smiled, as if that pleased him. "The dragon god will not return to you tonight, Zara, so you may rest well. But keep your guard up during your journey. He will do whatever he can to make sure you do not reach your destination."

"Wait—" I started as he disappeared, but the light faded away until I was blanketed in warm, heavy darkness. The exhaustion lurking at the edges of my mind hit me like a tidal wave, and after four days of terrible sleep, I gratefully allowed it to drag me under.

SIX

"You look like you had a good night of sleep," Tavarian said as we dressed for breakfast the next morning. He reached out and caught me by the chin, his strong fingers tilting my head as he studied my face. "The shadows under your eyes are all gone, and you look almost chipper."

"Caor visited me in my dreams last night," I admitted. When Tavarian quirked a brow, I hastily added, "Not like that. He was urging me to go to the forge." I filled him in on everything that had happened in the dream, and what Caor had told me about Salcombe.

"While it would have been nice if he had spread the dream love around, I am glad that you at least got a restful night's sleep." Tavarian caressed my cheek with the back of his hand as he smiled down at me. "You've been in low spirits the last couple of days, and the others have noticed. I think it will do them good to see you back to your usual self."

I smiled back, but a pang of guilt hit my chest as I traced the shadows beneath his eyes with my thumb. "Are you sure you don't want to rest for another hour or so?" I asked. "We should be able to manage without you for a bit."

"I'd never be able to lie abed knowing that everyone else is running around and being productive," he said ruefully. "However..." He slipped his hands down to my waist and slowly backed me up against the stone wall. "There is something else you could do that would give me a boost."

"Oh yeah?" My breath caught as he nuzzled my neck, and I slid my hands up the back of his untucked shirt to feel his muscles flex and ripple beneath my hands. "And what is that?"

Tavarian lifted his head, and the wicked gleam in his eyes made my skin tingle with the need to let him touch me all over. But before he could answer, someone pounded on the door.

"Commandant! There's been an attack!"

"Dammit!" I ducked under Tavarian's arm and yanked the door open. One of the sentries was standing in the hall, his face flushed as he panted. "What happened?"

"A group of soldiers went out into the hills for an early morning hunt. They'd made slingshots the night before and were going to try and bring down some birds and rabbits. But a band of fifty locals ambushed them. Several are badly wounded, and if there hadn't been a dragon nearby, we would have lost most of them."

"Shit." I raked a hand through my hair. "Where are the wounded?"

"In the infirmary, being treated."

"I'll be right down," I said, and slammed the door in his face.

Tavarian and I hurriedly finished dressing, then made a beeline for the infirmary, which had once been a large study back in the manor's glory days, or so Daria had surmised when they'd first arrived. She'd told me there were remnants of bookshelves and pieces of a broken desk left behind, and she'd even found a few pages from a history text lying on the ground. I was certain the owner of the manor had never imagined that one day in the future, all the furniture in his study would have been cleared out and replaced with bleeding soldiers lying on the ground, treated haphazardly by other soldiers with basic field medic training.

"Let me," Tavarian said, laying his hand on one of the medic's shoulders. He gently nudged the man aside, then knelt on the ground beside a woman whose abdomen was bleeding profusely. The other six men and women in the room all suffered similarly bad wounds.

"How many were in the party?" I asked the medic.

"Ten," he murmured. "Four of them only suffered minor scratches, but these..." He glanced helplessly at the other patients as he lowered his voice. "Well, if not for Lord Tavarian helping out, I'm not sure they would make it."

We watched as Tavarian slowly healed the wound, his face contorted in concentration. I wished I could comfort him or do something to help him shoulder the burden—he always felt pain when he healed a wound like this.

"It is his burden to bear," Lessie said sympathetically. *"Just as the dragon god's heart is ours."*

"I take it you know about the dream?" I asked her.

"Yes. I overheard you telling Tavarian about it this morning." In a pained voice, she added, *"I wish I could do something to help, but I battle the dragon god in my own dreams, too."*

"It's all right," I said, though I had to wonder. How powerful did someone have to be to be able to torment multiple people's minds at once? I honestly couldn't fathom it.

"The real question is how twisted do you have to be," Lessie said darkly. *"The sooner we can destroy that thing, the better I'll be able to sleep at night."*

"Literally," I added, and she chuckled.

The woman Tavarian healed fell asleep instantly, her body working hard to replenish the blood it had lost. I couldn't question any of these guys for a while, so I asked the medic to take me to the ones who had escaped relatively unscathed and questioned them about the encounter. Most of them said they had no idea which family the attackers had come from, but one woman said she thought they were from the settlement on the western end of the island.

"They wore these dyed blue strips of leather as arm bands," she said. "I've seen those a few times on that side of the island, back before we realized it wasn't safe to wander around."

I thanked the woman for her information, then called another meeting.

"It's probably the Porcillas family," I told the others as we sat cross-legged on the floor. "The natives we spoke to said that they've declared blood vengeance upon us because we killed two of their members during the airship attack."

"I've had enough of this," Halldor growled, banging his fist against his inner thigh. "We can't just sit around and let them continue to attack us like this—they'll just think we're weak. We need to show them our strength and intimidate them into backing down."

"That may make things worse," Tavarian warned. "The natives said that once blood vengeance is invoked, it can't be called back until the blood debt has been satisfied. Attacking them may just result in them adding to the blood debt they perceive is owed."

"Then we'll just have to do it without killing anyone," I said firmly. "We're not barbarians. Surely we can figure out how to intimidate them without actually shedding any blood."

We spent the next thirty minutes formulating a plan, then gathered a team of five and set out to where we thought the Porcillas family was located. As the settlement on the western end of the island came into view, I slipped my goggles over my head and counted the number of houses dotting the hilly area.

"Around three hundred or so," Lessie said. *"Those men were right. It is a very large clan."*

"Maybe, but they've clearly never prepared to deal with dragons." I pointed to the largest house, which was perched on the top of the tallest hill in the region. Normally that wouldn't matter, as the entire village was surrounded by a canyonlike moat on three sides, making it nearly impossible to access by normal means except by a single rickety bridge that was well-defended. *"Like most leaders, they've chosen to stick their most important building out like a sore thumb. And it's going to cost them."*

I lifted my hand in a signal, and as one, the five of us dove for the clan chieftain's home. As we approached, arrows zipped through the air, but Tavarian raised his left arm and conjured a magical shield. The arrows bounced off the large, glowing blue orb as it flickered to life around us before falling back to the ground and their befuddled owners. I grinned as the locals stared at us, slack-jawed, as we soared past them, and my smile only widened when my treasure sense finally pinged loudly.

"The weapon!" Lessie crowed excitedly. *"It has to be."*

All four of us landed at the top of the hill, forming a perimeter around the house. It was three times larger than the ones around it, but still a rather basic wattle and daub construction. The dragons moved closer to the house to form a tighter circle, and Tavarian took a minute to strengthen the magical shield before we approached the front door.

"Chieftain," I called as I banged on the door. "Open up. We need a word with you."

When no one answered, Halldor kicked the door open and stormed inside, sword out. Three men were waiting in the large entryway, swords drawn, but Tavarian waved his other hand and conjured a strong gust of wind. The miniature gale knocked them back into the wall hard enough to rattle their skulls, and the men slumped to the ground, unconscious.

Halldor glanced over his shoulder, an astonished look on his face. "I didn't think you could do two spells at once."

"It takes some effort," Tavarian said, a bead of sweat sliding down the side of his face. "But you looked like you were about to run your sword through that man, and we agreed on no killing."

Halldor's face flushed, but I pressed on through the entrance and into the next room, and they followed in silence. I kept my dragon blade extended as far as the space would allow, using it as a sort of deterrent. We encountered two more men who would have jumped us if not for the risk of impaling themselves on my blade, and Tavarian used his magic again to knock them out.

"These weapons are of considerably better quality than the ones the Ariban men carry," Halldor murmured as he paused to examine one of the swords.

I nodded. "If they managed to get to the estate before the other clans, they would have taken the better weapons."

We turned a corner, then stepped over a threshold and into a kind of receiving hall in the back of the house. It was an open space with packed dirt floors covered with rushes. Light filtered in from thin rectangular windows lining the tops of the high walls. Since they had no glass, they couldn't afford to have large windows. A huge fireplace dominated one side of the room, and on the other was a raised platform. The chieftain stood in front of a rough-hewn wooden chair, a huge bow and arrow trained on my face, while four women sat around him on pillows, glaring hatefully at us. The bow, like the other weapons, was of much better quality than anything I'd seen on the island so far.

"Chief?" I asked the man standing in front of the throne. He was a hard-edged man, dressed in a rough-spun kilt shot through with dark blue thread, and boots that looked like they'd been repaired several times. Swirling blue symbols peeked out from the neckline of his long-sleeved shirt, and a puffy scar slashed over his left cheekbone.

The chieftain bared his teeth in an angry snarl. "Give me one reason why I shouldn't put this arrow through your throat."

"My name is Zara Kenrook," I said calmly, even though my heart was beating an anxious tattoo in my chest. All it took was for him to release his hand on that string, and both Lessie and I were dead. "I am the leader of the dragon riders who have taken over the estate you attacked last week. We have come to negotiate a truce and settle any grievances between both parties."

"I am Chief Cramus," the chieftain spat back, "and we do not do truces. "You have invaded our land, killed two of our people, and—"

"The land we are currently occupying is not yours," I said, cutting him off sharply. "It is not part of your territory, and is closest to the Ariban Clan's territory, so if anyone has the right to be angry at us, it is them."

"It was our goats that your dragons killed, not the Ariban Clan's! And you have not provided reparations for the stolen goats." The chieftain curled his upper lip. "Now if you have nothing else to say—"

"If you release that bow string," Tavarian said in a voice like ice, "I will order our dragons to lay waste upon your entire village. You may have more men, but I assure you that your spears and arrows are powerless against dragon fire. They will burn down your entire settlement before you can fight your way through us and escape this house. And you will be trapped at the top of this hill with your wives and children."

A flicker of movement caught my eye, and I glanced sideways to see a blond little boy peeking through a curtained door. My heart squeezed at the sight of his chubby little face, and I sincerely hoped we wouldn't have to resort to anything drastic. The thought of killing innocent women and children... of actually massacring... we couldn't go through with it. If the chieftain refused to back down, we would just have to leave and hope the next island we landed on was more welcoming and not under enemy control.

The chieftain, whose face had been ruddy with anger, paled as the magnitude of Tavarian's threat sank in.

"You wouldn't," one of the women on the floor cried. "You wouldn't tell your dragons to kill us all. We are Elantian-born, just like you!"

"Exactly," I said gently as I met the woman's tearful eyes. By the shape of her mouth, I could tell the boy staring at us was her son. "And I know your ancestors were treated horribly by the dragon riders who left you all here, but we are still the same nation. I promise we'll do whatever we can to help your people, as soon as we can get what we need."

"It's always about what you need," the chieftain growled. "What about what we need?"

"Our needs are the same," I said firmly. "We are searching for a weapon that we believe is in your house, a weapon we need to defeat an enemy that has taken over the country. These people are trying to kill and enslave our dragons, and it is only a matter of time before they come for this island. When they do, your people will not be spared."

"What enemy is this?" The chieftain's voice echoed with shock as he finally lowered his bow. "No one has ever defeated dragons in combat before, never mind taken the country."

Tavarian and I explained about the war between Elantia and Zallabar, and the superior weapons the enemy was using. "The only reason we came to this place is because we heard the last dragon riders who were living here hid a powerful weapon somewhere on the island," Tavarian said. "We have reason to believe that it is here in your house. When you looted the larger estate, did you find anything that looked like a weapon?"

The chieftain's brow furrowed. "We confiscated many swords and axes, yes," he said, "but nothing like what you mention."

"Chief Cramus," I said, trying to put this as tactfully as I could. "I have a special ability that allows me to sense items of great value, and ever since we approached your village, I have sensed a very valuable piece here." Closing my eyes, I drew on my treasure sense and conjured up a smoky image of a large ivory horn carved with ancient runes. I described it to him. "Do you have anything in your home like this?"

"We do," the chieftain said, sounding puzzled. "But that is a battle horn, not a weapon. It makes a fearsome sound when you blow on it, but nothing beyond that."

My heart sank a little. Could it be nothing more than a horn? "Even so," Tavarian said, "we would like to inspect it. I may be able to translate the runes, which might have specific instructions regarding the use of the horn. Perhaps it needs to be held at a certain angle or blown in a specific manner."

"Wait a minute." The woman sitting to the chieftain's right rose, placing a hand on her husband's bicep. She was a voluptuous woman with black-as-night hair, and she glared at us with icy blue eyes. "If we give these people the horn, there is no reason for them not to run off with it. Why should we part with an object of such value without receiving anything in return? And they still haven't satisfied the blood debt!"

"We do not acknowledge a blood debt," Halldor said hotly. "It was you who attacked us, not the other way around. What we do acknowledge is a goat debt, which we promise to make good on once our ship is repaired and we can go get supplies to offer you in payment."

The woman and Halldor glared at each other for a long time, a stalemate neither was willing to give up.

"We do not wish to fight with you," I said in the tension-filled silence. "But we cannot leave without that horn."

The chieftain sighed, finally sitting down in his chair. "Then let us negotiate."

He snapped his fingers, and the servants brought us pillows to sit on while we talked with the chieftain. The negotiation went quite a bit better than expected, but the fact remained that the chieftain refused to give up the horn without receiving something in exchange.

"I cannot just call off the blood debt, either," he said. "If I do, the other clans will think we are weak, and they might join forces against us. The only way that we could consider the blood debt settled without killing two of yours in return would be to receive a gift of extraordinary value. And before you think to offer me gems or gold, don't bother. We have no use for any of that on this island."

"Then give us a week," Tavarian said. "Let us call a temporary truce while we collect the payment owed. If we do not return with it in a week, then you are free to resume your attacks. Though," he added darkly, "we cannot say what will happen when we are forced to defend ourselves."

We left the chieftain's house feeling if not triumphant, at least relieved.

"How are we going to get what they need within a week?" I asked as we flew back to base. "The airship isn't going to be repaired in time."

Tavarian smiled. "Maybe so, but we don't need an airship for this." He waved his arm around us. "We have dragons."

SEVEN

"Are you ready for this?" I asked Tavarian as we strapped on our armor. The sun hung low in the sky, bleeding red through our tower room window, the color oddly appropriate considering what lay ahead of us. I hoped it wasn't an omen. We couldn't afford to lose any more riders, not when Zallabar was already doing such a good job of killing us off.

"I'm actually quite looking forward to it," Tavarian said, tugging a gauntlet into place.

"Are you?" I studied him for a moment, admiring the way the silvery scales on his armor flashed red in the dying sun. An image of him riding Muza flashed into my head, and I wondered if Tavarian was thinking of his dragon now. The two of them would look formidable charging into battle together, but Muza had essentially taken a pacifist vow, refusing to fight in Elantian wars any longer. Since they were both bound by law to serve in the dragon rider force, that meant Tavarian had been forced to fake Muza's death and send him off to some faraway place, where he would never encounter other dragon riders.

"Yes." He gave me a bemused smile. "Though I did sincerely abhor the war that Muza and I were forced to fight in, this is different. Elantia may have committed wrongs against Zallabar in the past, but Zallabar is hardly innocent, and it does not justify them trying to conquer our country. If we don't take action, they will only use our wealth and resources to take over more countries until they've conquered the entire continent. Besides," he added with a shrug, "we are not actually going into battle this time. This is a stealth mission."

"Now made more complicated because we need to bring back sacks of grain and supplies as well as treasure," I said with a sigh. "Are you sure we're not trying to take on too much? The longer this takes, the more likely we're going to get caught."

"We don't really have a choice," Tavarian said. "Either we get the supplies to appease the Porcillas family and trade for the horn, or we return empty-handed and they attack us again. The other riders and dragons will only take so much abuse, and the last thing I need is for us to end up setting the entire island on fire and unwittingly destroying that weapon."

"Yeah." I winced at the image that conjured—this place was so dry I could easily see that happening if the dragons got too riled up. "All right, let's get everybody together."

We went down to the field, where the teams we'd organized were already forming. We'd added a fourth member to each of the three teams, including ours, to help collect supplies for trading, bringing our total number up to forty-four.

I approached Rhia and Jallis, who were on our team. "You

guys ready?" We were taking the most dangerous mission—infiltrating Zuar City—which was why I'd opted to have Rhia and Jallis by my side instead of heading up other teams.

"Yeah." But Rhia's face was tight. "I don't know what we're going to find, though. I can only hope that my mother already got out with our dragon egg, but..."

"Your mother is a smart woman." I placed a hand on Rhia's shoulder. "I'm sure she's fine." But secretly, I worried, too. It wasn't just rescuing Rhia's dragon egg we had to worry about; our primary mission was to retrieve the piece of heart Tavarian had hidden. And that was hardly the half of it. We needed to haul as much gold away as possible, check on Rhia's mother and my friends, and possibly rescue Jallis's cousin Dyron. Dyron and his parents were not dragon riders, so they'd been living in a middle-class neighborhood in Zuar City. Hopefully, they'd escaped the notice of the Zallabarians, but there was always a chance they would take the boy in the hope that he would hatch a dragon for himself.

Even so, I was secretly relieved to be leaving the island, even if it was just for a few days. Thankfully, I didn't have to worry about how the men would fare. It had been three days since the officers among Ragorin's troops, especially the sergeants, had taken the organization of the base in hand. They were a lot better at it than the dragon riders. Cooking and cleaning were well organized, as was the fishing and numerous other operational considerations that I hadn't even begun to confront. Even the locals were starting to cautiously barter with us. The men we'd spoken to earlier must have said something to convince the others it was worth trying to establish some kind of relationship.

"Commandant." I turned at the sound of Captain Ragorin's voice. He was approaching us with thirty soldiers in tow. "These are the men and women who will be accompanying you on the journey."

"Great." I surveyed the group, all dressed in civilian clothes. Ragorin himself had suggested the idea of bringing them along. The idea was that they would be re-inserted into the country as civilians, with different identities, to help build up a resistance against Zallabar and eventually throw out the invaders. They stood straight-backed and stern as Ragorin introduced them, and though they looked grim, I could sense the determination in their hearts.

I took a minute to get to know each of the men and women, wanting to learn a bit about them before I sent them off into a mission that many of them might not come back from. One of them, Lieutenant Kinley, told me he used to be a merchant sailor, and I quizzed him about the island where the Forge of Derynnis was located.

"I don't know anything about a forge," the soldier said, "but there's only one volcanic island in that part of the ocean, and no sailor would dare go there. There's no fresh water, and it's way too far from any shipping lanes to be useful."

Wonderful. "How far is it from the closest port?" I asked anyway. It didn't matter how hospitable the place was—we weren't going there for a vacation.

"Twelve days minimum by ship, if the wind blows fair, but up to forty if you're unlucky. If that happens, you'll probably run out of food or water. I highly advise against going there, Commandant. The likelihood is you won't survive."

"Noted." I supposed that situation suited Derynnis. He was the god of death, after all.

As I continued to question him, pulling out as many details about the place as possible, Lessie and I quickly realized it would be impossible to fly to the island. It was too far for any dragon to make the flight in one go, and dragons couldn't float on the open ocean. We would all drown.

"Great," Lessie grumbled. *"That means we're going to have to travel by ship again."*

"Nobody said this was going to be easy." But I sympathized with Lessie on this one. I didn't have a problem traveling by ship so much as I hated having to rely on one. Ever since Lessie and I first started to fly together, the power of flight had given me a sense of freedom I'd never experienced before. The two of us could go anywhere the wind could take us...except, apparently, to an ornery death god's secret forge. The realization was more than a little humbling, or in Lessie's case, infuriating.

But we'd have to worry about that later. Right now, we had more immediate concerns to attend to.

After checking in with each team and making sure they understood the orders, our team took flight. Tavarian rode with me, while Jallis ferried our extra passenger, Lieutenant Diran. She was a petite woman, small enough that I doubt Kadryn noticed the extra weight on her back, but the gleam I'd caught in her eyes when she'd introduced herself told me that what she lacked in size, she made up in attitude and willpower. She was just the person we needed on the ground in Zuar City, stoking the fires of rebellion.

The flight was long, nearly four hours, but with Tavarian's

cloaking spell to shield all four of us, it felt almost like a leisurely outing rather than a stealth mission. With Tavarian's warm body at my back, the glimmering ocean beneath us, and the twinkling stars watching from above, I allowed myself to relax for a little while and enjoy what felt like a stolen moment.

"Are you missing Muza right now?" I asked Tavarian as I leaned back against him.

His answer was muffled, his nose buried in my thick mass of hair as he leaned his chin against the top of my head. "I actually had contact with him recently."

"Really?" I sat up a little straighter. "Were we close to his hidden lair?"

"Not at all," Tavarian said. "Muza and I have a way of communicating despite the distance between us. It is a kind of lucid dreaming, but it only works if both of us are trying to reach out at the same time. Sometimes we can sense fluctuations in emotion that tell us when we need to make contact, but oftentimes we miss such cues, and when that happens it can take weeks for us to catch up. In this case, Muza sensed my recent worries, and he reached out."

"What did he tell him?" Lessie asked eagerly. *"Is Muza coming out to help us?"* Lessie was very fond of the older dragon and had missed him terribly once they were forced to part ways.

I repeated the question and felt Tavarian shake his head. "He offered, but I told him not to come. As much as I miss him, one more dragon is not going to change the outcome of the war. However," he added, "I did ask him to meet us on our way to the forge, since his lair is in the far south anyway."

"What do you know," Lessie said. *" I have something to look*

forward to about this trip after all. Muza's company will make things more tolerable, even if we have to sit aboard that stupid ship."

"*You'll still be able to stretch your wings and fly,*" I pointed out dryly. "*You'll just have to come back to the ship before you tire out.*"

"Is Muza's lair near the forge, then?" I asked Tavarian.

"Oh no, it is at least a thousand-mile journey, if not more." Tavarian chuckled wryly. "I thought that Muza's location was remote, but it is somewhat accessible if you know what you're looking for. But Derynnis has us beat, that is for certain."

"You think he's a crotchety old man, hunkered down in the middle of his volcano as he works on…well, what does he work on?" I asked. "If it's a forge, does that mean he makes weapons?" There were a few legends about ancient weapons forged by the death god, but they were few and far between, and I'd never heard of anybody actually finding one. "You'd think if he did make them, there'd be a few more around."

"Perhaps he does not wish to share his creations with the world," Tavarian said, sounding amused. "Though one does wonder at a death god creating anything, even if his creations are not living things."

Jallis and Rhia were having their own conversation as we flew, but as we finally crossed into Elantia, we all went quiet. With only the stars to light our way, we could hardly see anything at all, but from this high up the landscape seemed unchanged. My heart swelled at the sight of familiar forests and rivers, fields and valleys, rippling below us, and for a moment I could almost pretend we were on a training flight and we'd be back at Dragon Rider Academy any minute now.

Despite Tavarian's cloaking spell, we made sure to avoid larger towns and cities as we headed for the capital. The moonless night meant we had to fly slower than usual, looking out for any patrolling airships. Thankfully, there did not seem to be very many, which bolstered my confidence that the floating islands might yet be intact.

"We'll stop here for the night," I said to everyone, indicating a thickly wooded forest just ahead. We were about two hours' walk from the capital still, but I could feel Lessie's flagging strength through the bond. "The dragons can rest here, and we'll head in tomorrow morning."

As it turned out, finding a spot for all three dragons to land was a bit of a challenge, considering we needed to keep them hidden. We found a section of the forest tucked beneath a huge rocky overhanging cliff, and the dragons used their brute strength to clear away some of the trees to make the space wider. It was large enough for all of us, and we could climb up the cliff if we needed a better vantage point of the city.

As we laid out our bedrolls, a male voice asked, "Getting ready to settle down, are we?"

I whirled around. Caor stood just beyond the tree line, his form enveloped by a soft glow.

"Tsk, tsk," he said, glancing at the huge stack of felled trees. "Such a waste of timber. Are you sure you need those dragons?"

Lessie, Ykos, and Kadryn turned their heads simultaneously toward Caor, low warning growls rumbling deep in their bellies.

But the messenger god only laughed, tossing his long, honey-brown hair as if he didn't have a care in the world.

"Try me," he taunted. "Your claws will only grasp air."

"Can we all pretend that we're on the same side for a minute?" I snapped as the dragons gnashed their teeth. Rhia and Jallis were of no help. The two of them gawked at Caor like idiots. "Why don't you get to the point and tell me why you came here?"

"To warn you, of course." Caor's expression turned deadly serious. "Salcombe is on his way to Zuar City as well. He wears a new face, and with his acolytes still in the city to assist him, he may yet beat you to your goal. You must hurry."

"Great." I groaned at the thought of having to square off with Salcombe yet again. "Can't you tell us what disgui—"

But Caor was already gone, leaving me in the dark both literally and figuratively.

EIGHT

The next morning, the five of us set off for the city, each headed in a different direction. We'd risen before the sun so the dragons could drop us into better positions before going back into the nearby woods to hide themselves. Rhia, Jallis, and the lieutenant we were planting were headed in through the southern gate, while Tavarian and I took the north.

"This thing is heavier than I thought it would be," I huffed as Tavarian and I pulled a cart laden with hay. We'd filched it from an abandoned farm, which I'd hated doing but hoped the owner wouldn't mind too much. It was for a good cause, right?

"Thankfully, we won't have to worry about lugging it out again," Tavarian said. "We can leave it at the market, or perhaps with one of your orphan friends to sell."

"That's a good idea." I'm sure life was harder on everyone since the Zallabarian occupation had begun, and someone would appreciate the free hay. "I wonder how the Treasure

Trove is doing. I can only guess that sales are suffering since the Zallabarians have chased all the nobles out of the city."

A massive line, at least a quarter-mile long, already waited outside the gates—both pedestrians here to visit friends or family, and merchants who commuted to the city daily on carts to sell their wares. Tavarian and I joined the end of the queue, and I had to stifle a sigh of impatience as we inched along. As we got closer to the gates, I saw the hold-up. The guard around the gate had been doubled, and every single person was being stopped, questioned, and if they were bringing a cart or other vehicle, searched.

As we got closer to the front of the line, sweat beaded on my forehead. What if they decided to search me? I'd left my dragon blade behind out of necessity, knowing it was far too conspicuous as a dragon rider weapon, but I had plenty of knives strapped on. Had the Zallabarians enacted a weapons ban? I wished we had a better idea of what to expect.

We were only five people away when an elegant carriage rumbled past us, kicking up dust along the way. I scowled as it stopped right in front of the gates, cutting ahead of everyone else who had been patiently waiting.

"What gives?" I complained to Tavarian as one of the guards approached the carriage. The passenger opened the window, and my frown deepened as a young dandy with sky blue eyes and riotous blond curls leaned out to talk to the guard. There was a brief but pleasant conversation, and the guard scribbled something on a small sheet of paper, then pulled it off his clipboard and handed it to the man.

"Perhaps he's a government official?" Tavarian asked. "Though he does seem rather young."

The line moved quickly after the carriage passed through the gates, and in no time, we were at the front. To my relief, the guards did not try to pat down either Tavarian or me when it was finally our turn for inspection. After giving them our cover story—we told them we were going to visit my sister after selling the hay—the guard handed us a two-day pass, then waved us through without a backward glance.

"Two days is more than enough," Tavarian said as we pushed the cart through the bustling city streets. As we made our way to the orphanage, I studied the buildings for any outward sign of resistance. At first nothing seemed amiss, but as I looked closer, I noticed things out of place. Broken windows in nice neighborhoods, boarded-up storefronts in what were normally thriving shopping districts. But even worse were the constant presence of Zallabarian guards. There was a guard posted in every square, every public avenue, and I knew they were the cause of the undercurrent of tension running through the city.

"I wonder how many citizens they've had to kill to keep the peace," Lessie said as she observed through my eyes. I didn't miss the low-level rage simmering in her voice. *"A handful? Dozens? How can anybody expect to fight back against those horrible weapons?"*

Lessie was referring to the pistol and rifle each guard carried. *"We're going to need to get our hands on some of those 'horrible weapons' ourselves,"* I reminded her. *"If we're going to *have any chance of defeating Zallabar, we have to embrace new technology."*

Lessie only grumbled.

We made a quick stop at the market to buy bags of produce, then went straight to the orphanage. "Thank you for your generosity," Miss Cassidy said fervently as we handed the cart and its contents off to the grateful staff. "We have been surviving well enough on the supplies you provided us before you left the city, but that won't last much longer."

"Why not?" I asked. "Are prices so high you can't afford to buy more?"

"No, it's not that," she said heavily. Her spindly body sagged into her chair, and every line and wrinkle seemed to weigh on her face. "The funding we received from the government, meager though it was, has been completely cut off, along with all other grants the former government was previously paying. The new leadership wants to go through everything with a fine-toothed comb, but during this time of transition all funding has been cancelled. Only the rich have been able to get their projects approved, and no one seems to care that in a matter of weeks, we will all be turned onto the street."

The bitterness in her tone reminded me of my early years at the orphanage. The place had barely had the funding to put a roof over our head. Many of us had been forced to beg, or in my case, steal, in order to get by, especially if we wanted any spending money. I'd thought it was a terrible existence, but at least I'd had a place to lay my head at night. If the new regime took that away, they would soon find their city streets littered with the bodies of sleeping or dead children.

Anger bubbled inside me like a hot cauldron, and I clenched my fists in my lap. "What about appealing to the upper class?" I asked. "They were the ones who helped get the orphanages on their feet in the beginning, weren't they?"

Miss Cassidy shook her head. "Most of the rich in this city are dragon riders, and as such they have been chased out of their homes and are as poor as us now," she said sadly. "And that's if they haven't been arrested. The ones who aren't nobility don't have a care for us at the moment. They are too busy squabbling over what land and houses haven't been occupied by the general and his officers."

Tavarian and I exchanged grim looks. "I was afraid something like that might happen," he said. "So, the new nobility is making common cause with the Zallabarians?"

"Very much so," Miss Cassidy confirmed. "So many houses have been vacated that the new government is selling them off cheaply, and the new upper class is very happy that the dragon riders have been chased off to make way for them. They fancy themselves the new ruling class." The distasteful look on her face spoke volumes about what she thought of that. "While I've always had my issues with the way the dragon rider class ran things, at least we had a system I could count on, even if we could only count on it being unfair. Now we don't know what is going to happen." To my horror, tears sprang to her eyes. "And the worst of it is that this building itself was owned by a dragon rider family. We've been leasing it from them for decades, but now these greedy local investors want to grab it and will most likely raise the rent. Not that we could afford even the nominal amount the previous owner charged with our funding cut off."

"I'm so sorry," I said as she pulled a handkerchief from her skirt pocket and dabbed at her eyes. I couldn't blame her for crying. Six staff members and over thirty orphans lived here, some of them only toddlers. "Lord Tavarian and I aren't going to be here very long, but we'll see if we can find a solution."

"Thank you." Sniffling, she tucked her handkerchief away, then tried to put on a brave smile. "And even if we don't, we are still grateful for your help, Zara. I am sorry for whatever differences we may have had in the past. You have been a true friend to the orphanage."

Though Tavarian and I left the orphanage with heavy hearts, my spirits lifted again as we made it to the Treasure Trove. To my pleasant surprise, the shop was still intact, with plenty of wares on display.

"They must still be doing good business," Tavarian said as we entered the shop.

Carina, who was ringing up a large and expensive-looking porcelain vase, nearly dropped the priceless item when we walked through the door.

"Za—" she began, then cut herself off, remembering that I was a wanted woman. "Kira, would you mind helping this wonderful lady with her purchase? There's an urgent matter I need to attend to."

"Of course, Miss." Kira stared at us with wide eyes full of delight as Carina ushered us into the back, and I promised myself I'd take a minute to catch up with her and Brolian before we set off again. After all, we had some time. The dragon heart relic was hidden in a public building that we would have to wait until nightfall to break into, as it would be crawling with Zallabarians right now.

Once we were safely away from prying eyes, Carina threw her arms around me in a vise-like hug. "I'm so happy to see you're still alive," she said on a half-sob, and I hugged her a little tighter as she trembled in my arms. "But what are you two doing here, Zara? Dragon riders are being rounded up left, right, and center for execution. It isn't safe for you here."

"Hence the farmer's wife getup," I said wryly as I pulled away to indicate my outfit. "Tavarian and I make a cute couple, don't you think?" I looped my arm through his and used my free hand to snap at the suspender strap running over his left shoulder.

That stunt earned me a snort from Carina and an eyeroll from Tavarian. "Yes, it's a brilliant disguise, except for the fact that anyone who knows you will recognize your face immediately," she said. "If only we hadn't sold that blasted fan, you could have used that to disguise yourself as a hag again."

My shoulders tightened as the fan reminded me of Salcombe once again. Was he already in the city? The fan couldn't change that wiry build of his, or the fact that he now moved with preternatural speed and grace thanks to the power of the dragon god, but he could assume any face he wanted, even a woman's if he wore the right clothing. I would have to be on guard for any sighting of him or his acolytes.

"I'm very happy the shop has managed to keep its doors open," I said, wanting very much to change the subject. There was nothing I could do about Salcombe—we'd find out tonight if he'd already beaten us to the punch. "I gather more of the new nobility has decided to come shopping here to fill the empty halls of their newly purchased mansions?"

"Well, yes," Carina admitted, her cheeks flushing. "But we've also had a surprising amount of business from the Zallabarians. It turns out the general himself has a penchant for ancient artifacts and vintage items."

"I bet," I murmured, thinking of General Trattner and his family once more. He would have loved my shop, and I wondered if he would come to Zuar City one day. The irony of him standing in my shop, admiring the wares, after I'd stabbed him in the back multiple times was almost too much to bear, so I cast the thought aside.

"Seriously, though, Zara, what are you two doing here?" Carina crossed her arms over her chest. "And please don't tell me you brought Lessie with you."

"She's not in the city, of course, but yes, she's around. How else did you think we got here?" Briefly, I told her about the stealth mission, and more specifically, our role in the city.

By the time I finished, Carina's face had turned white. "So Jallis and Rhia are here too? That means you have not one but three dragons nearby."

"Is there something we need to know about, Carina?" Tavarian pressed. "Something other than the obvious?"

Carina sighed. "The Zallabarians are especially angry at dragons right now. The airship that was ferrying over our new governor exploded en route. Apparently, the governor's entire household was aboard, as well as quite a lot of gold, so they're understandably pissed about it."

Tavarian raised an eyebrow. "Any chance the explosion was a malfunction?"

Carina shrugged. "It could have been, but the Zallabarians are inclined to think a dragon brought the ship down."

"Well, well," Lessie said smugly. *"That sounds like a familiar story, doesn't it?"*

I gasped as the memory surged into my brain. "Where did the airship explode, exactly?" I asked Carina.

"Somewhere near the Zallabarian border. Why?" she asked sharply.

"Yeah...that was us," I said, a little sheepishly. "Lessie and I were scouting when we encountered the airship, and we figured we might as well bring it down while we were out. We figured they were ferrying weapons or supplies."

"They probably were doing that, too," Carina admitted, "but your act of heroism has definitely made things harder back home. Ever since the explosion, the Zallabarians have become very paranoid. They've tripled the guard, enacted an eight o'clock curfew for anyone not carrying a special pass—and if you're not rich or Zallabarian, you can't get one—and other bullshit regulations that are pissing everyone off."

"A pissed-off population is a good thing, right?" I asked. "After all, if our citizens are resentful toward the new regime, they're more likely to respond favorably to a revolt."

"Yes, but many people are blaming the dragon rider class and the former regime for the stricter measures," Carina said. "It's not fair, I know, but people will lash out at whatever they can to make themselves feel better about the situation, and you and Lessie would be the obvious target if they knew you were responsible. The truth is, despite all the unfairness going on, almost nobody wants the dragon riders back."

"Well, they're going to get us back, regardless," I said grumpily. "I didn't go through all this work just to be spurned by my own damn country."

"I know." Carina laid a hand on my shoulder. "And I'll do whatever I can to help you. But the two of you need to be especially careful not to let your dragons be seen. The Zallabarians will kill them on sight."

After that depressing bit of news, Tavarian left to scout for tonight's mission. I stayed in the back while Carina returned to the front of the shop, inspecting the wares and polishing up newer finds. Our stores were looking a bit emptier than usual, and I imagined that was the result of the Zallabarians' stricter measures. Treasure hunters would have a harder time traveling in and out of the city with curfews and gate checks, especially since many of us liked to smuggle in illegal items to sell along with our more legitimate wares. I had a feeling the Zallabarians would be no less tolerant of drugs or other contraband than the Elantian officials had been.

I was just inspecting a jeweled scabbard when the door banged open and Rhia raced inside.

"Mrs. Thomas!" I exclaimed as Rhia's mother rushed in behind her. The two of them looked quite out of breath, both clutching large, heavy bags to their chests.

"What's going on?" Carina demanded as she followed in behind them. "Why do these two look like they've been running from the muncies?"

"Because of this," Rhia said as the two women set down their bags. She opened the smaller one, and I gasped as she pulled out a golden dragon egg. "We didn't want to be caught with it on the street."

"Dragon's balls," Carina swore, her eyes bugging out of her skull. "Do you have any idea what will happen to me if the guards find that thing in my shop?"

"Our shop," I reminded her, "and it won't be staying long. We're rounding up all the eggs we can find and taking them out of the city, remember?"

"Right." Carina eyed the egg warily as she raked her hand through her long, black hair. "Well, let's hide that thing in the cellar for now," she said. "Don't need someone walking back here by accident and finding it."

As we did so, rolling the egg up in cloth and tucking it inside a sack of grain, Rhia and her mother told me what had happened.

"I was chased out of my family home, as were most dragon rider families," Mrs. Thomas said, "but because I was not a rider myself, I was lucky enough to merely be thrown onto the street rather than imprisoned. Thankfully, I have friends who live only two blocks away, a middle-class family who worked with our shipping company for many years, and they agreed to take me in. Rhia, smart girl that she is, thought to look for me there."

"And not a moment too soon," Rhia said hotly. "Danton, the son of the family Mother was staying with, found out she was hiding the egg in her luggage and had arrived back home at the same time to take it from her. I had to knock him out in order to get away safely, but it's only a matter of time until he wakes up and gives the guards our description."

"And then there will be posters all over the city with sketches of your faces," Carina said with a groan. "Wonderful."

"I'm sorry to be so much trouble," Mrs. Thomas said. Tears shone in her eyes, and her lower lip trembled a little despite her efforts to keep a brave face. "It's just that I couldn't bear to leave the egg with him, not when the Zallabarians have made it their mission to exterminate all our dragons."

I thought about telling her our theory that the Zallabarians were planning on using the eggs to create their own army, but decided now was not the time. "No one is blaming you, Mrs. Thomas," I said, and put an arm around her shoulders in what I hoped was a comforting embrace. "You did the right thing. My friends and I have come back to Elantia for the express purpose of rescuing the eggs, so we're very glad you brought this one to us."

The four of us retreated upstairs, and Carina went to the front of the shop to flip the open sign to closed so we could discuss the best way to smuggle Rhia, her mother, and the egg out of the city without being detected. But we'd barely begun the discussion when Carina walked back in, and she was not alone.

"Jallis!" Rhia and I jumped to our feet at the same time, but she beat me to him. "What on earth happened to you?" she asked as she caught his bloodied face in her hands. Jallis winced as she tilted it this way and that to inspect him. His left eye was purpling, his lip split, and from the way he was hunched in on himself, I suspected he had a few bruised, if not broken, ribs.

"I did a stupid thing," he groaned as Rhia helped him limp to one of the few chairs in the back office. The agony written all over his face made me wish Tavarian were here to heal him, and for a second, I wished Muza were here so the two of us could communicate via dragon.

Carina rushed to fetch the medical kit I kept in the apartment upstairs while Jallis told us what happened. He'd decided it would be a good idea to enter his own family's townhouse on Dragon's Table to try to recover a few valuable heirlooms they kept there. Unfortunately, the townhouse had already been occupied by Zallabarians, who had called the guards immediately upon finding an intruder.

"They called the guards on me like I was some kind of vagabond and had me beaten before they threw me out on my ass," Jallis growled, his eyes bright with anger. "Off my own property!"

"You're lucky that's all they thought you were," Carina scolded as she applied ointment to Jallis's cuts. To his credit, he didn't even wince—I knew firsthand how much that stuff stung —but that might have been because he was too angry to notice. "If they knew you were the former owner's son, they would have arrested and executed you for sure. Your life isn't worth a few trinkets."

Jallis's hands fisted in his lap. "I just can't stand the idea that the enemy is living it up on my family's property." But then he let out a sigh, the fight going out of him. "At least my parents weren't actually there, though. I hope they stayed on the floating island. It's very well defended, so they should be able to hold out for a few days."

If the Zallabarians don't use their airship cannons to blow it to pieces, I thought, but didn't want to worry Jallis by mentioning it. Besides, I had a feeling the Zallabarians would refrain from doing that unless absolutely necessary. They would want the islands as intact as possible, after all.

"Zara," he said wearily, catching my hand in his. "Would you mind heading over to my cousin's house for me and checking on him? I don't think I can make it there in my condition."

I held in a sigh as I surveyed the room. One reluctant-to-help best friend, one too beat up to walk, and two who'd already managed to get themselves on the wanted list. Yep, this definitely boded well for tonight's heist.

"Sure," I said, putting on a brave smile to hide my very real worry that this was all about to go up in flames. "That should be no problem at all."

NINE

Jallis's cousin's house wasn't hard to find. It was some thirty blocks away, in a middle-class neighborhood that was considered if not the nicest, at least one of the safest parts of town. It was also largely untouched, since there were no dragon riders or people of importance living here. The houses, painted in conservative shades of blue, green, and brown, looked the same as they always had, and there were even mothers walking about with their children, taking them for strolls or to the park to play.

Of course, there were still guards patrolling the streets, just like everywhere else. But they seemed more relaxed here, almost indolent even. The people in this section of town had already fallen in, and why shouldn't they? From what Carina had told me, there had been only nominal shifts in the economy. I'd figured there would be an outright collapse, with dragon riders owning so many of the businesses, but since they'd been using normal middle-class people to help run their enterprises, things continued on much as they normally did. Sure, there might eventually be changes in regulation that would impact things, and the curfews and gate checks probably slowed things down some.

But the people who lived here didn't need to worry about these problems. As long as there was someone else in charge to see to the details, they could continue living their suburban lives as if the country hadn't been turned upside down.

I knocked on the door of the address Jallis had given me, and a woman in her thirties with a baby on her hip answered the door.

"Can I help you?" she asked, looking me over suspiciously. I supposed she had a right to be suspicious. After all, it wasn't every day that country folk wandered into suburban areas, and I was still playing the part of farmer's wife.

"I'm sorry to bother you, ma'am, but I'm looking for the Tibas family." I gave her what little details of Jallis's family I knew. "I come to the capital every year and always visit my cousin Tibas while I'm here, but I can see they're not in residence. Have they moved?"

The woman wrinkled her nose. "The family who was living here abandoned this house," she told me. "I assume they were dragon rider sympathizers and had to flee the city to escape the guards. Which was lucky for me and my husband," she said with a shrug. "We bought this place dirt cheap."

I had to bury my anger at the woman's attitude. She didn't seem at all sympathetic to the plight of the house's previous occupants. "Are you sure you don't know where they went?" I injected a note of desperation into my voice. "If my cousin and his family are in some kind of trouble, I need to know."

"My suggestion is stay far away from your cousin if you know what's good for you," she warned. "If he's really a dragon rider sympathizer and you're caught with him, you could get arrested too." Her eyes sharpened as she looked at me. "Unless that kind of affliction runs in the family, and you deserve to be arrested."

"N-no, of course not," I stammered, holding my hands up as I backed away. "I have no love for dragons or their riders. I can't tell you how many times they've stolen sheep from my husband and me as they've passed by my farm, and we're expected to just take it, too!" While that story wasn't mine, it was not, in fact, a lie. I'd heard similar tales from others about dragon riders taking advantage of them, and I knew that despite my outrage at the way the people were behaving, they had reason to hate the riders. If we ever did take back our country, things would definitely have to change amongst riders and the common people. There would no longer be a purely dragon rider council, for one thing. The ground-dwellers needed to have fair representation, too.

The woman nodded sympathetically, her suspicion melting away. "I'm sorry to hear about your plight," she said, "but I'm sure things will improve for you and your husband now that the new regime has taken over." The baby on her hip started to fuss, and she bounced him a little, cooing softly. The abrupt demeanor change from shrewd suspicion to motherly love was startling, but her expression turned businesslike once more as she turned back to me. "Now if you don't mind, I really need to get back to my day."

"Of course." I inclined my head. "Thank you for your help."

I knocked on a few other doors, just to be sure, and found out from one neighbor that Jallis's cousins left to stay with "relatives in the countryside." Unfortunately, they'd left no forwarding address, but I had to assume that was a good thing, and that they'd reached some kind of sanctuary. I resolved to speak to Lieutenant Diran and see if she and the other plants could establish some kind of underground network for the dragon rider families who had escaped persecution. If we could band them together in common cause, that would put us one step closer to taking the country back.

TEN

"Well, we look quite different," I said as Tavarian and I inspected each other. Once we'd returned to the shop—and Tavarian had healed Jallis—the two of us assumed rather drastic disguises using clothes and a makeup kit Carina had purchased for us. Tavarian was dressed as a humble clerk in an ill-fitting waistcoat and breeches, his long hair twisted and tucked beneath a dusty cap. I used makeup to soften his angular features and dotted his hands liberally with ink spots. "I don't think anyone looking at you would guess that you're a dragon rider, never mind a former Elantian ambassador."

"And I don't think anyone looking at you would think you were a treasure hunter," Tavarian said with a crooked smile. I was posing as his wife once again, this time in a drab gray dress that looked more like something Miss Cassidy would wear. My own curly red hair was tucked under a brown wig that I'd twisted into a knot at the nape of my neck, and I'd used makeup to give myself a dull, pasty appearance. "You'll have to keep those eyes lowered, though," he murmured as he caught my chin in his hand. "I'd recognize those striking blues anywhere."

My heart beat a little faster as I stared into Tavarian's swirling silver eyes, which were hidden behind a pair of spectacles. "Look who's talking," I murmured, my body instinctively swaying into his.

Our lips met, and I closed my eyes for just a second, trying to pretend we were a normal couple enjoying a simple moment of domestic bliss. His mouth was soft and warm against mine, stoking a lazy flame of desire inside me, and when he flicked his tongue against my lower lip, I nearly moaned out loud.

"A promise for later," he said as he drew back, his eyes burning with lust. "When we make it through this."

I nodded. The moment we returned to Polyba, safe and sound and with eggs and treasure in tow, I was going to jump his bones. It was the least I deserved after all we'd been through.

"Are you sure you don't want us to come with you?" Jallis asked as we went downstairs to make our goodbyes. "It feels wrong to send the two of you up there alone, especially after what happened to me."

"No," Tavarian said. "We need to stick to the plan, and besides, there's no time for us to put disguises together for either of you."

"Besides, we're not breaking into someone's home," I assured them, "and it'll be nighttime, so fewer prying eyes. Trust me, it'll be okay." I touched the amulet, which was hidden beneath my dress. I didn't expect it to protect me, as it only worked against magical attacks, but it was a comfort to have all the same.

Get going, Caor's voice echoed in my head. *You don't have much time.*

Tavarian and I hastily finished our goodbyes, then hurried to the base of Dragon's Table, which was perched on top of a giant mesa at the edge of the city. "It's been a while since I made this trek on foot," I puffed as we climbed the twentieth flight of stairs. Only forty left to go, right?

"You've climbed these before?" Tavarian asked from behind me. Like me, he was slightly out of breath, but I was thankful we both stayed in good enough shape. The stairs zigzagged up the side of the mountain, with platforms at various intervals for people to get on and off the elevators. I generally preferred a straight shot up, but many people, especially tourists, liked to get off at different elevations to enjoy the view.

"Yes, back when I didn't have a pass." Only those who lived or owned businesses on Dragon's Table were given them. The rest of us had to hoof it. I'd eventually gotten one myself from Barrigan, the antique shop owner I used to treasure hunt for, but when I'd quit, it had been revoked. I hadn't gotten another until I became a dragon rider.

Maybe the rules have changed, I thought as I glanced askance at the lift tracks. Both lifts were hanging at the top of the mountain. It wasn't past curfew yet, but it was late enough that people wouldn't be coming and going anymore. Once upon a time, the sons and daughters of dragon rider families would have been hopping on and off these lifts, heading away from their privileged lives to enjoy a night of debauchery in the lower city, but there was none of that now. The people who had moved into the houses up here already knew what life was like on the ground, and I doubt they wanted the reminder.

Though guards were posted at the different platforms, they let us pass with barely a glance. *They probably think we're silly tourists or something, hiking up all these stairs just for a glimpse at the city view.* Which was fine by me. The less memorable we were, the better.

When we reached the top, I wanted to take a moment to catch my breath, but the moment I set foot on Dragon's Table, a faint but familiar gong echoed in my head.

"You sense it already," Tavarian said, recognizing the look in my eyes. "I used a spell to muffle the signal, but if you can sense it, Salcombe will be able to as well. We should hurry."

I allowed Tavarian to take my hand and pull me along through the quiet city streets. We passed through a shopping district I was quite familiar with, and my lips pursed as I noticed Barrigan had moved his shop to a larger, grander building than the one he'd been in before. *I bet he'd moved into one of the dragon rider mansions, too,* I thought. Barrigan had always been a favorite amongst the nobility, but he was a snake, and I'm sure he had no problem ingratiating himself with the new regime once he saw which way the tide was turning.

But thoughts of Barrigan and my old life quickly fled as Tavarian led me into a warren of old buildings, the upper city's historic district. The dragon heart's signal tripled, humming loudly in my skull, and I wanted to arrow straight toward the location only a few blocks away.

"And what business do the pair of you have up here on Dragon's Table?"

I forced myself not to freeze at the guard's voice.

"Good evening," Tavarian said pleasantly as we turned to face the pair of guards that seemed to melt out of the shadows. "My wife and I are in town visiting for a few days. Her sister, Anna, is a cook for a family that lives on Primley Drive, and we've come to visit now that she's off shift."

He presented the pass we'd collected at the gate, and the guards inspected it for a long moment. For an anxious second, I was worried he might not give it back, but finally he handed it over.

"Curfew's in two hours," he said shortly. "See to it that you've concluded your visit by then."

"We will. Thank you."

I could feel the guards' stares on our backs as we continued down the street, so Tavarian and I ducked into an alehouse on the corner, a cozy but low-key establishment that catered to just such servants as the fictional sister we were visiting.

"We'll wait here until the patrol passes," Tavarian said as we sat down at one of the few empty tables. A buxom woman in a form-fitting tavern dress came over to take our order, and we both got tankards of ale. I sipped at my mug cautiously, mostly for show. The brew was good and strong, but we couldn't afford to get buzzed, not when we were about to break into a government building.

As Tavarian and I made small talk, the door opened again, and the young man with the riotous blond curls walked in. He looked around the tavern, his blue eyes sweeping the busy crowd before he walked up to the bar to order. I didn't expect the flicker of recognition when he looked my way—after all, he wouldn't have noticed me amongst the crowd outside the gates—but to my surprise, his gaze narrowed on me before he turned away.

"Don't you think he looks suspicious?" I murmured as I leaned closer to Tavarian. "Look at those fancy threads. He doesn't belong here."

Tavarian glanced at the man. "He seems harmless enough," he said after a minute. "Just a young dandy wandering about town. But if he worries you, we'll keep an eye on him."

But as we watched, the young man didn't do anything suspicious. He simply sat at the bar and chatted up the man next to him while he worked on his mug of ale, and he never looked my way again. By the time he ordered a second mug, Tavarian tugged on my arm, and we slipped into the dark streets once more.

"Nearly there," he said under his breath as we navigated through several unlit back alleys. We had to move more slowly to avoid the patrolling guards, and as we crouched behind a group of trash cans, I wished for Halldor's ability to sense people. My treasure sense could come in handy sometimes in that regard, but in the middle of a city with so many objects of varying value, it was impossible to pick out a soldier from anyone else.

We came to a stop in front of an unobtrusive door at the back of an ancient house crammed between two others almost exactly like it. After checking to make sure no one was watching, I fished my magic lock pick out of my skirt pocket and slid it into the keyhole. One quick twist and we were inside, my spelled boots muffling my footsteps while Tavarian used whatever spell he had to move ghost-like through the house.

"This way," he whispered, so quietly I almost didn't hear him. We made a sharp left, then went straight downstairs to the cellars. Tavarian used his magic to conjure a small, glowing orb.

I stopped dead as the light illuminated a large space filled not with caskets of wine or stores of food, but thousands upon thousands of boxes.

"Correspondence and files from past diplomatic missions," Tavarian explained as he led me to a stack in the corner. "The cellar houses old archives, and the floors above contain the more recent records. Thankfully, the librarians and record keepers only work during the day, so there should be no one within."

My treasure sense told me the piece of heart was tucked not in one of the boxes, but beneath them, so I helped Tavarian move the stack of boxes aside so he could get at it. A plank of wood beneath popped free easily enough, and I held my breath as Tavarian lifted a spelled box out of the hole.

"I'll be taking that," a voice I'd know anywhere said, and I froze.

"Salcombe," Tavarian said flatly as he straightened, box in hand. "It would seem Zara was right to be suspicious of you."

I turned around and gasped. He was the young man we'd seen in the tavern! "You've been following us all along," I accused.

"But of course," Salcombe said with a shrug. It was highly unsettling to hear his deep voice echoing out of the throat of a young man. In his last disguise, he'd always spoken in a Warosian accent, since we'd been posing as nobles from that country, but there was no need for such deception now. "Why expend the effort when I can just ride on your very capable coattails?" He gave a sigh that was downright theatrical. "It's really too bad you had to be so obstinate, Zara. You were an apt apprentice, and we could have done great things if only you would cast aside your foolish morality and join me."

"Yeah, I think I'm good," I said, and threw a dagger before I finished speaking. That trick usually worked. People were generally too focused on what you were saying to notice you were already attacking, but Salcombe dodged in a blur of motion. I palmed another knife, but he barreled into me before I could even think which way to aim, his hand on my throat as he slammed me into the wall.

"Get off her," Tavarian snarled. He ripped Salcombe away, then used his magic to throw him across the room. "Take it and run, Zara!" he cried, tossing me the box.

I caught it one-handed and raced for the door, but Salcombe appeared in front of it.

"You can leave once you've handed it over," he said pleasantly, but Tavarian hit him with a powerful gust of wind, slamming him into the wall before he could wrest the box from me. I half-hoped he might slump to the ground, unconscious, the way the Polybans had done when Tavarian had performed the trick earlier, but no such luck. Salcombe rebounded off the wall and launched himself at Tavarian, his face twisted with fury.

"Enough of this," Salcombe roared, raising his hand. Tavarian blasted him with more wind, and my heart shot into my throat as black flames shot from Salcombe's hand. The wind whisked the magical fire through the room, and in seconds the boxes were ablaze.

"Damn!" Tavarian swore as he raced for the door, but the flames had already spread to block it. Salcombe cackled, an evil sound that turned my blood to ice, and I glanced back to see him standing amid the flames, his hands raised as he basked in the destruction he'd created. The flames licked at his clothing, but he seemed unaffected, and I imagined the dragon god's influence was protecting him.

Magical fire. Right. "Take my hand," I yelled. "We can do this!"

I seized Tavarian's wrist in mine, then dragged him toward the door. The flames leapt high, licking at the ceiling, but I reached through them anyway, grasping the door handle. It was hot enough to burn, but the amulet I wore flared to life, preventing the flames themselves from latching onto my clothes.

Salcombe's laughter turned into another snarl of rage as I flung open the door, but Tavarian blasted him back with another gust of wind before he could catch us. Heart racing, I slammed the door shut and stuck my lock pick into the handle, then twisted it the wrong way to magically seal the door.

"That's not going to hold him for long," Tavarian warned. The flames were already eating through the doorway. Salcombe would be on us in a moment. "Run!"

We sprinted up the stairs, my amulet still blazing with light as we ran through the flames. The fire was eating up the entire house, and as we got farther from the basement, it turned from magical black to mundane red. Shouts dimly rose from outside over the roar of the fire as the fire brigade and soldiers arrived.

Tavarian and I burst outside through a servants' entrance on the side of the house, gulping in great lungfuls of crisp, cold air. We glanced around to see if there was a way to sneak off, but the brigade was already here.

"Get back to the lower city," Tavarian whispered, his voice harsh from smoke inhalation. "I'll distract them."

I wanted to protest—getting separated was not part of the plan—but he was already running toward the firefighters. "Did you see them?" he cried. "The masked men who set this place on fire? Surely they must have run right past you!"

I leapt over a hedge as Tavarian concocted whatever wild story he'd come up with, slipping the small box into my skirts to settle with the other piece of heart. The feeling of wrongness doubled, slithering over my skin like an oily caress, but I forced myself to keep moving, heading for the Blue Daffodil. My friend Portina ran the place, which was why we'd agreed on it as our pre-arranged meeting point. If things had gone wrong and the authorities came looking for us, she would hide us and keep our secret.

"Hey," Portina greeted me as I walked in, careful not to say my name aloud. I'd sent a note ahead telling her to expect me so that she wouldn't give me away with her surprise. She was behind the counter as usual, pouring ale and spirits, but I noticed she'd taken on two new bar hands to help her out. It wasn't hard to see why. The place was packed, more than I'd ever seen it before. "What can I get you?"

"Just an ale for me, and another for my friend." I wedged myself into the sliver of available space between two men so I could lean in and talk to her. "Looks like business is booming around here."

She smiled as she poured my drinks. "All of the lower-end establishments like mine are," she said. "The soldiers have taken over the classy joints, so this is where normal folk go to get away and pretend like we aren't under occupation." She slid the mugs over to me, then frowned as I placed a coin on the counter. "Your money's no good here."

"But—"

"No." She slapped it back into my hand, then made a shooing motion. "You can pay me back by doing what you came here to do. Now get going. I have customers waiting!"

Stifling a grin, I wound my way through the crowd and found a small, empty table toward the back of the room. As I sat back in my chair, eyes trained on the door as I sipped my ale, my thoughts drifted back to the last time I'd been here. I'd been ruminating over a mug of ale at the time too, trying to figure out what my next move was, when Jallis had shown up. The two of us had been at odds—I barely remembered what about, now— but he'd given me my dragon blade that night, and he'd stuck by my side as I solved the mystery of Tavarian and his dragon heart piece. Whatever Jallis and I had gone through, I would always be grateful to him for giving me that piece of my identity, the one object that was a tangible link to my real family.

My fingers twitched, seeking out the two-ended blade now, and I sighed, remembering I'd left it back in Polyba. It was too risky for me to carry a dragon blade in Elantia. They were extremely rare, ancient weapons once wielded by dragon riders. The mages who'd crafted them keyed them to the families they belonged to, so they could only be wielded by those who had the right blood. The fact that the blade had responded to me when I'd picked it up had been unmistakable proof that I'd come from a dragon rider family. Unfortunately, the family crest that had once adorned the handle was missing, and without it there was no way to tell who.

Will I ever know? With the Zallabarians mercilessly hunting down the dragon riders, it was all too possible that my real family, whoever they were, would be wiped out before we took the country back.

If we take the country back, a small voice in my head reminded me, but I shoved it ruthlessly aside. I couldn't contemplate the possibility of failure. Not when the accompanying future was so bleak.

I was saved from my thoughts by Tavarian entering the pub, looking flushed but no worse for wear.

"Everything turn out okay?" I asked as he sat down in the chair across from me.

He nodded, then took a great gulp of ale before speaking. "I distracted them with a wild tale about staying late to work and seeing a group of masked men set the fire through a window overlooking the back garden. The authorities are now convinced that the arsonists were a group of patriots fighting back against the Zallabarians."

I bit my lip. "I hope the fallout from this isn't going to be too bad." The regime would likely enact even stricter measures, and would probably make an example of anyone they could to discourage further acts of violence. I hated that people would suffer for what we'd done, but there was nothing for it.

Retrieving the dragon heart before Salcombe could was of paramount importance.

"I'm guessing we're going to have to put the second part of our plan on hold?" I asked.

He nodded grimly. "It's too dangerous to consider going back, and curfew is almost here." We'd been planning on hitting the treasury, but since it was on Dragon's Table there was no chance of that now. "Our priority is to get the relic—and our friends—away from here as fast as possible. There's no telling when Salcombe will try to come for us again."

I nodded, tension digging into my shoulders again. I was surprised Salcombe hadn't already caught up with me. Was it possible he'd been injured in the fire? I knew the black flames couldn't hurt him, but the fire could have brought wooden beams or other heavy objects down onto him, and I had locked him in the cellar.

But whatever injury Salcombe had suffered wouldn't keep him down for long. The dragon god had invested too much into him. He wouldn't let his champion fail now.

ELEVEN

After deciding it was too risky to return to the Treasure Trove—Salcombe could very well have told his local minions about our presence, and that was the first place they'd check—Tavarian and I finished our ale and headed for the orphanage.

"We need to hurry," I said, my breath frosting in front of my face as we hustled through the emptying streets. "Curfew is almost upon us."

We expected to arrive at a quiet scene—the orphans would be settling down for bed at this hour—but what we encountered was quite different.

"You can't do this to us!" Miss Cassidy shrieked as she was dragged from the building by two rough-looking men. "We have nowhere else to go!"

"Then you shoulda come up with the rent money when Mr. Blighton asked for it," the thug sneered as he tossed her aside. I darted forward to catch her just before she fell, and the man sneered at me. "This ain't none of your business. Now move along."

I ignored him, helping Miss Cassidy back to her feet. "I thought you said that the investors were still haggling over the place?" I asked her as the staff and orphans were marched out of the building. Half of them were in their nightclothes, clutching what little belongings they had to their chests.

"It turns out the building was purchased this morning." The words came out as a sob, and my heart plummeted to my toes as the children began crying as well. "When Mr. Blighton's representative came tonight, I told him that we didn't have the funds to pay the rent. I asked for more time, to see if we could raise the money we needed, but these men won't hear of it."

"Where are we going to go?" one of the older orphans asked, a boy no older than eleven. His teeth chattered as he clutched a threadbare blanket around his thin shoulders, and his wide eyes were filled with more worry than any child should have to experience. "The soldiers will throw us in prison if they find us on the streets now."

"At least prison will offer a warm place to sleep," one of the other kids muttered. Her cheeks flushed red when Miss Cassidy glared at her. "What? I'm just trying to stay positive."

"You're not going to prison," I announced firmly to the group, wanting to squash that notion before it could take root. "I'll find you guys a place for the night, and we'll go from there." Turning to Tavarian, I added, "I'll take them back to the pub, see if Portina can put them up for the night. Meanwhile, do you think you could talk some sense into these guys? I know we can't move the children back in, but there's no reason for them to hold onto the stores of food or any other belongings left behind."

"I'll do my best," he promised.

"Thank you." I turned back to the orphans and staff and raised my voice over the anxious din to be heard. "I need everyone to form two lines, quickly! We don't have much time."

The staff managed to marshal the orphans into some semblance of order, and we marched down the street, back to the Blue Daffodil. Thankfully it was only a few blocks away, and we made it back with two minutes to spare.

"Tavern is closed!" the bouncer announced as he tossed two drunks out onto the street. "Besides," he added, his eyes narrowing, "we don't accept tykes their age here."

"We're not here for drinks," I told him. "Please, go get Portina. She's expecting me."

That last bit was a lie, and for a minute I was worried she wouldn't come, since I couldn't give my name. But Portina appeared at the door soon enough, and her annoyed expression gave way to one of astonishment when she surveyed the crowd camped outside the door. "Miss Cassidy!" she exclaimed. "What in the bleeding skies is everyone doing here? Is this the entire orphanage?"

"It is," she said tightly. "I hate to impose on you like this, Portina, but we are in desperate need of your help."

Portina sighed, eyeing the approaching guards. Their fingers were twitching toward the whips at their belts, and my own hand unconsciously reached for one of the daggers hidden in my skirt even though I knew it was pointless. "Let's get you inside before these fools decide whipping children is acceptable behavior, and you can tell me all about it." She trained a gimlet stare on Miss Cassidy, and I knew she was remembering all the times we'd gotten our knuckles slapped with rulers, or were bent over the knee and spanked, because we'd broken the rules.

Miss Cassidy's cheeks reddened, but she merely lifted her chin and ordered the others to follow her inside. Thankfully, the establishment could hold up to fifty people, so we all crowded in at the tables, and I told Portina everything that had happened, including my friends' various plights, in the privacy of the back room.

"I'll send a runner to the Treasure Trove first thing in the morning," she promised. "As for the orphans, they can bed down here in the tavern. I'll bring what extra bedding I have from upstairs, but I warn you, it's not much. You'll all have to sleep on the floor."

When we emerged back into the public area of the tavern, I was relieved to see Tavarian amongst the group.

"Did everything turn out okay?" I asked, rushing over to check him for any bruises or bumps. He was unscathed. Surely the guards would have tried to arrest him for being out past curfew, wouldn't they?

"I managed to convince the men to allow the orphanage staff to come and collect their stores in the morning," Tavarian said. "Believe it or not, the guards actually assisted with the issue. Seems they were thankful not to have to round up a bunch of children and toss them into prison overnight, and they upheld my view that by law, the new owners had no claim to any of the property within the walls since the orphanage did not owe them a debt."

"Lucky for us the Zallabarians are mostly pragmatic." Of course they wouldn't actually want to beat and arrest the children. That would only cause public outrage and make it harder for them to establish control over the city. While they were applying a vise-like grip on the citizens now, they knew that sort of thing wasn't sustainable. Eventually, they wanted the public to settle down and accept the new regime so things could resume some semblance of normalcy.

The orphanage staff were overjoyed to hear that they were being allowed to collect their belongings, but their fears were far from allayed.

"It is very kind of Portina to let us stay the night," one of the staff said, "but what about tomorrow? Where will we sleep, and where will we store the supplies once we get them?"

"I'm afraid you will all have to leave the city entirely," Tavarian said. "The two of us do not have the time or resources to help you find a new residence in the city, and you know what will happen if you all end up on the street tomorrow night."

"Leave the city?" The staff looked like they were about to keel over from shock. "But I've spent my entire life here!"

I squared my shoulders. "Look, I know you guys are just employees here, and you probably have families to go home to. If any of you want to leave, to head back to them, you're more than welcome." I pinned Miss Cassidy with a frank stare. "I sincerely hope you're not one of them. Someone needs to be around to take care of the children." And even though Miss Cassidy and I had different ideas on how to handle small humans, she was the only one with experience, and most importantly, the only one here.

Miss Cassidy straightened her spine. "Of course I will come with the children," she said. "Just because the government has cut off funding does not mean I can abandon my responsibility to them. Besides, I have no family here in Zuar City. It's just me." She turned to the staff. "While you are free to leave in the morning, I must say it is going to be a challenge caring for over thirty children by myself. If any of you would like to volunteer to come with me, I would greatly appreciate it."

Most of the staff didn't look enthused about the idea, but two stepped forward, an older man with a thick silver mustache and a lean build, and a young, dark-haired woman who couldn't be more than twenty. I knew both of them. The woman was Tammy, a former orphan who'd stayed on both because she liked children and because there was nowhere else to go. The man was Filan, the cook. The food he made was barely fit for consumption, but I knew that wasn't really his fault— the scarce funding had restricted us to mostly gruel. I was certain that with the additional supplies, he'd been making better meals for the kids. They didn't look nearly as scrawny as the ones I'd grown up with.

"I don't mind coming with you," Filan said. "My children are all grown and moved out of the city, and my wife passed two years ago. But I am reluctant to leave when there is no guarantee of a new place to call home. What do you have in mind?" He turned to Tavarian. "Do you expect us to camp in the woods?"

"No," Tavarian said. "I have a few ideas, but I need to confirm some things before I can announce anything. For now, we should all try to get some sleep. I will update everyone in the morning."

I pulled Tavarian aside as the staff helped the children settle down for bed. "What's your plan?" I asked. "Do you want to take them to the hidden estate?" It was definitely big enough to house everyone, but how would we get everyone there? The dragons couldn't carry more than three or four people at a time. They would have to make multiple trips, and the others would be forced to camp out somewhere in the meantime. And what if bandits or thieves came upon them? Not to mention that we didn't have time for this. We needed to get back to Polyba as soon as possible to make that trade with the Porcillas family.

"No, that would be too difficult logistically," he said. "However, my floating island is set to arrive here in a day or two, which means it is only an hour's flight from here."

"Right." Tavarian had a device that told him where his island was, a combination of magic and technology that tracked the magnetic pull of the island. "So we can just fly them up there. We'll have to wait until nightfall tomorrow, though, and that'll still be risky as hell." Tavarian's cloaking spell only worked if the dragons were high enough in the air. Too close to the ground and they became partially visible. "Do you think they'll be safe up there? Considering how pissed the Zallabarians are about that airship crash, I'm surprised they aren't patrolling the skies more regularly."

"I imagine the autocrator is having his engineers work on a new airship design, something more dragon-resistant," Tavarian said. "As we've demonstrated, it is far too easy for dragons to take out the airships, and too costly to continue sending them out only to have them destroyed. To be honest, I have no idea how the Zallabarians will create a design that is truly dragon-proof."

"They don't have to," I said bitterly. "All they need to do is exterminate the remaining dragons and bring the newly hatched ones under their control, and it won't be a problem anymore."

With little else to do, Tavarian and I retired for the night, sleeping on the floor with the others. Once more, I was plagued by terrible nightmares, and was woken up repeatedly by children crying.

Damn you, I cursed the dragon god silently as I held a four-year-old in my arms, trying to rock her back to sleep. It was one thing to torment me, or even the fellow riders who were helping me, but poor, innocent children who had just lost their home, who had no families?

"It's unforgivable." Caor's voice echoed in my head. "And the longer you delay your journey to the forge, the more people around you will suffer."

I chased Caor's words around in my head for most of the night, the restlessness and anxiety having long banished any possibility of sleep. Besides, I had a feeling that as long as I stayed awake, depriving myself of rest, Zakyiar would have less hold over the dreams of others around me. The theory seemed to hold true—none of the other children woke again. Even Tavarian seemed to sleep deeper, his breathing normal.

Great, I thought absently as I stroked a hand down his back. His powerful muscles flexed a little, but he did not wake. *So, all I have to do is stay awake until we reach the forge and I destroy the pieces of heart. Easy.* I fingered the amulet resting against my chest, wishing it could do something to protect me against the dragon god's dreams. But I had a feeling it could only defend against magic in the real world. That, or Zakyiar was too powerful, even in the spirit realm, to be stopped by something as simple as an amulet.

The moment the first rays of sunlight began to poke through the windows, I forced myself from the hard ground and went upstairs to wake Portina and get her to send a message to the Treasure Trove.

It didn't take long for an answer. A mere two hours later, just as the children stirred from their own pained slumbers, Carina filed into the pub with Rhia, Jallis, and Mrs. Thomas in tow. "I'm so glad you're all right," Carina said as she threw her arms around me, and I was shocked to feel her tremble a little as I hugged her tight. "When you guys didn't come back to the shop last night, I was terrified that you'd been caught and that I would see you two swinging from the gallows today."

"I'm sorry we couldn't get a message to you sooner," I said, then pulled away to inspect the others. "We barely made it off the streets in time for curfew as it was. Did anything unusual happen last night?" I asked Rhia. "Anyone come to the shop looking for you or your mother, or the dragon heart?"

"As a matter of fact, a man did come by early this morning," Carina said grumpily. "Some stuffy official who claimed he needed to search our place for contraband. I was worried he'd come searching for Rhia and her mother, so they hid in the cellar. But he didn't seem to be looking for a person, at least not that I could tell."

"What did he look like?" I probed.

"Mid-forties, lean, posh," Carina said. "Red beard."

A chill ran down my spine. "That's one of Salcombe's acolytes. He must have come to see if I was hiding out at the shop with the piece of heart we nabbed." I glanced sideways at Tavarian. "Guess it's a good thing we didn't go back to the shop after all."

He nodded. "It's only a matter of time before Salcombe's men come looking at other places of interest, like this one," he said. "We need to get out of here, but I'm not sure how to make that happen since we were unable to break into the treasury last night."

"I believe I can assist with that." Carina gave me a crooked smile as she hefted a giant purse from the pack slung over her shoulder. "Your half of the profits," she said, handing it to me. "With a bit of an advance, since I know I won't be seeing you for a while."

My mouth dropped open as I took the bag. Judging by the weight, it held a small fortune. "You don't have to give me all this," I said weakly. "Surely you should keep some for when the shop goes through lean times. It's bound to happen soon."

But Carina shook her head. "We've got plenty squirreled away for rainy days," she said. "I don't think you quite comprehend just how much we've made since you became a dragon rider. And even though I've given you money here and there, for the most part you haven't even had a chance to enjoy the profits. I wish you were taking this money to buy yourself a nice house on top of a hill for you and Lessie to enjoy," she added with a sigh. "Not spending it on this terrible war."

"Perhaps I still will buy that house on a hill, when all of this is over," I said lightly. I only hoped that hill was somewhere in Elantia, and not in a foreign country where we would have to hide from the Zallabarians, forever fugitives.

The six of us sat down together while the staff got the children up and dressed for the day, then hashed out a plan. Carina and Portina left with some of the gold to procure carts and donkeys, while Tavarian and I accompanied the staff to the orphanage to collect their belongings. Thankfully, only two thugs guarded the premises today, and they begrudgingly let us pass. I wished we could take the furniture—there were lots of usable beds, desks, and other pieces—but aside from a few chairs, we stuck to the essentials and loaded everything on the carts Carina and Portina brought.

Miss Cassidy looked at the row of carts. Three of them were stuffed full of supplies, while the children sat atop boxes and crates. "I have to say," she said shakily, "in my thirty years of running the orphanage, I've never felt quite so overwhelmed."

"There, there." Rhia's mother put an arm around the woman and steered her toward the cart. "It will be all right. You have two wonderful people who've agreed to come with us, and I will be helping you as well."

I glanced at Rhia, who gave me a sad smile. "My mother always wanted a big family," she said as Mrs. Thomas darted around the cart, giving hugs to the children who were scared and making sure they were as well situated as possible. "But my father's death prevented it. We may have lost everything, but for her, this is a blessing in disguise."

The rest of us hopped into the cart at the front, and

Tavarian took the reins. He urged the two ponies into a quick walk, and we headed for the east gate.

The soldiers were sympathetic at the sight of so many small children, and to my relief, they barely spared the adults more than a cursory glance. "Wish I could say you were the first to be chased out of the city," the guard said gruffly. "But you're not, and you won't be the last. Best of luck to you all."

The soldier's unexpected empathy caught me off guard, but others in the cart weren't so easily manipulated. Jallis glared at the guards as we passed, and I had to squeeze his arm tight to keep him from doing anything stupid. He looked like he wanted to leap out of the cart and strangle the man. Rhia, Mrs. Thomas, and Miss Cassidy stared straight ahead, refusing to acknowledge them, and the staff kept their eyes lowered.

In other circumstances, I would be furious too. But I was too tired to summon the energy necessary for so much anger, so it was all too easy to let it go instead.

The children were quiet for most of the journey, in low spirits after being kicked out of the only home they'd ever known. I doubted any of them had ever set foot beyond the walls of Zuar City, never mind traveled through the Elantian countryside, and many of them stared dully as we passed barren fields and lonely farmhouses. The harvest season was long over, and a pang hit my chest. Zuar City always had a wonderful festival to celebrate, and that would have been a month ago. Though I doubted anyone had celebrated. Would there be any sort of celebration for winter solstice? The Zallabarians had their own traditions. Would they force them on us? Considering that many of our festivals and rituals centered around the dragons, I doubted they would let us continue with our own.

It took us only two hours to reach the forest where the dragons were hidden, but we had to slow considerably to navigate the narrow paths not meant for carts and horses. The animals whinnied nervously as we approached, sensing the giant predators, and Jallis jumped out of the cart to soothe the animals.

"It's all right," he cooed as he patted the horses' necks, stroking their damp hides and murmuring soothing words as they stamped their hooves. "No one is going to eat you today."

"Eat us?" one of the children cried. "Why would anyone eat us? What's going on?"

"You'll see," I said, twisting around in my seat to smile at them. "It's a surprise!"

This didn't seem to allay the children's fears, not that I could blame them. The horses' anxiety naturally affected them. Thankfully, Jallis managed to calm the horses using his talent, and we made it to a small clearing barely large enough to fit the horses and wagons.

"We'll need to leave them here for now," Jallis said. "Even my talent won't be able to calm the horses if they actually come face to face with Kadryn."

We left the orphanage staff to guard the horses, while Rhia's mother and Miss Cassidy led the children along to meet the dragons for the first time. Via Lessie, I ordered the dragons to lie low to the ground and be as non-threatening as possible. I needed the children to feel comfortable around them if we were going to ferry them up to the floating island.

"Dragons!" they cried, their sullen resentment and desperation evaporating at the sight of the huge beasts. I'd been worried the orphans would be frightened when we led them into the larger clearing, but although a few did seem nervous, most were excited.

"Oh my," Miss Cassidy breathed, her hand on her heart. The blood drained from her face, and she looked like she was about to faint. "This...is not what I expected."

"It's all right, Miss Cassidy." I gently took her by the hand and led her over to Lessie. She was nearly Kadryn's size now and had outgrown Ykos by a mile. "They won't hurt you."

Lessie fixed her fiery eyes on Miss Cassidy as we approached. *"Be nice,"* I warned as I laid the woman's hand on Lessie's snout. Her nostrils flared as she let out a huff, and Miss Cassidy jerked back as Lessie's breath clouded in the air around her.

The children, on the other hand, gasped excitedly, and soon enough one of them was tugging on my hand. "Can I try?" she asked eagerly, looking up at me with the biggest brown eyes I'd ever seen.

Before I could answer, Lessie shifted her head, nudging the little girl with her snout. The orphan giggled as she pitched forward, landing on top of Lessie's head, and something in my heart melted as she lay there, sprawled across Lessie's snout.

"So pretty," she cooed, running her little hand across Lessie's iridescent scales.

"I am nice," Lessie said smugly to me. *"Especially to little girls who acknowledge my magnificence."*

I hastily disguised my laugh as a cough before I turned to the children. "Anyone else want to try petting a dragon?"

"Me! Me!" Hands went up everywhere, and even Miss Cassidy had to laugh.

The children played with the dragons for the rest of the day while we waited for night to fall. I worried they might make too much noise and attract unwanted attention, but Tavarian cast a muffling spell across the clearing to mute their voices. As long as the children and dragons didn't set foot outside it, no one could hear them.

"It'll probably take ten trips to get everything to the island," I said to Tavarian and Jallis as we stood in the other clearing, inspecting the contents of the carts once more. "Do you think we should try taking the carts up, too?"

"I wouldn't advise it," Jallis said. "They're too unwieldy for the dragons to carry easily."

"We won't need them anyway," Tavarian said. "We can fashion litters from supplies on the island that the dragons can use to transport the supplies back down. It will take half the time for us to bring everything back down to the ground once we arrive at our destination."

"Excuse me," Miss Cassidy said as she entered the clearing. "I can't help but feel left in the dark. Where are you taking us with these dragons? It isn't as if it is safe to fly, even at night, when the Zallabarians are killing all dragons on sight."

"We won't be traveling on the dragons," Tavarian told her. "We'll be using my floating island."

Tavarian gathered everyone together, and we explained the plan. "It will take two days for the island to reach the hidden estate," he told them. "There is more than enough room for all of you to live there comfortably, and between what we've brought and the stores already there, enough food to last at least a year. There is a couple on the grounds to help with the cooking and cleaning, and a library with a selection of educational volumes you can use to teach the children."

The orphanage staff stared, their faces slack with astonishment. "An entire estate?" Tammy squeaked. "We thought perhaps you were going to leave us at a farmhouse or something."

"We are incredibly grateful for your generosity," Miss Cassidy said, "but what can we do for you in return? There is no way for us to repay you."

"You can repay us by teaching the children to be self-sufficient adults," Tavarian said. "There are books in the library about the history of the dragon riders, as well. Teach them the truth of it all—the good, the bad, and even the ugly. They are the future of Elantia, and they must not make the same mistakes we have."

When night fell, we mounted up, each dragon taking two children at a time in addition to the riders. Tavarian's cloaking spell kept us from being seen, and the children thought the short flight was great fun. Tavarian's staff were startled to see so many people arriving at once but relieved he was still alive. He quickly explained the situation while we got all the people and supplies situated.

Once everyone was settled, Tavarian and I went to his vault. "You know, I could do this faster with my lock pick," I joked as Tavarian spun a series of dials to open the heavy metal door.

He lifted an eyebrow. "That would trigger the alarm spell, and then we'd both be trapped inside here." He smirked as the door swung open. "Or have you forgotten what happened the last time you were here?"

"Right." I stepped inside, and a sense of déjà vu rippled through me as I looked around the room packed with valuable art and treasure. But despite the sheer amount of wealth in this room, my eyes went straight to the black lacquered box sitting on one of the shelves.

"So, it's still here," I murmured, picking it up. I flipped the latch up, opened the box, and stared into the empty space where Lessie's egg had once rested. Emotion surged in my chest as I remembered that fateful day, the thrilling combination of terror and elation that had erupted inside me when that egg had hatched, when I held Lessie's tiny body in my arms for the first time.

"It is." Tavarian squeezed my shoulder gently in support. "Do you want to take it with you?"

I hesitated, then placed the box firmly back on the shelf. "No, the dragons will be overloaded as it is."

"Then it will be waiting for us when we come back," Tavarian declared. I wished I shared his confidence in our return, then frowned at myself. Why shouldn't I be just as optimistic? Attitude tended to be the key difference between success and failure—I'd executed enough heists to know that.

"Yes, it will," I said, and then we turned our attention to the remainder of the vault. "There's enough treasure in here to fund a war campaign if we could sell all this stuff," I said, "but since there's no easy way to fence it, I'd suggest we just take all the coin and anything that's gold or silver that we can melt down or trade."

"Agreed," Tavarian said. "But we still need to figure out what we will give the Porcillas family in exchange for the horn." He tapped his chin as he considered. "Ferrying food to them will be awfully cumbersome, and now that we have the orphans, I am reluctant to part with any of that."

I considered for a moment, then remembered the bow the chieftain had trained on me. "You have to have an armory here, don't you?"

Tavarian's eyes brightened as he caught on to my idea. "Ah, yes. The weapons the Porcillas family took from the estate are the reason they have the advantage over the other tribes in the first place. It is only natural that they would want more."

We went to the armory, and sure enough, Tavarian had a sizable store of weapons—enough swords, shields, and daggers to arm at least two hundred people.

"Not enough to outfit the entire Porcillas tribe," I said as I balanced a dagger in my palm, testing the blade's weight, "but then again, I don't think I want to give them all weapons." The last thing we needed was for them to get cocky and try to come after us.

"Neither do I," Tavarian said. He drew a short sword and sliced through the air, nodding in satisfaction as he executed a few experimental strikes on an imaginary opponent. "It is not necessary to give them this many for a fair trade anyway. We should bring some for our own people, and perhaps hold on to a few to trade with the other tribes."

Great. So now we were becoming arms dealers. I wasn't exactly comfortable with that, but we needed that horn.

"That horn better be an actual weapon, or I'm going to be pissed," I muttered.

"You and me both," Tavarian agreed. He spun around and flung the blade across the room, where it sank straight into the center of a waiting target. The motion was graceful, effortless...and full of anger, I realized as I stared at Tavarian's clenched jaw. "You and me both."

TWELVE

The first night on Tavarian's island was the best night of sleep I'd had in a week. I wasn't sure if it was because the dragon god was too tired to bother me, or because we'd put the pieces of heart in Tavarian's magically sealed vault, but I slept through the night without a single nightmare.

"Mmm," I purred as Tavarian trailed warm, feather-light kisses down the back of my neck. His touch awakened a primal need inside me, and I arched into him, reaching back to skim my hand down his very naked thigh. "I could get used to this, you know."

His answering chuckle vibrated against the back of my neck, and sparks raced across my skin as he slid one hand up to cup my breast and the other between my legs. Foreplay quickly turned into a passionate bout of lovemaking, and I embraced the waves of pleasure as they rushed through me, clearing the cobwebs from my mind and filling me with buoyant optimism.

"I know we're still in enemy territory," I said as I lounged in Tavarian's embrace afterward. "But this is the best damn wake-up call I've had in a long time."

He laughed, his hand skimming up my bare abdomen. My skin tingled as he traced lazy swirls over my left hip, and my blood heated all over again. "We could go for a second round—" he started, but a growl from his own stomach cut him off.

I laughed as I patted his belly. "We have other needs to take care of. Besides, we should check in on everybody and make sure they're all right. The children have been through quite an ordeal."

"The housekeeper would have come to tell me if anything was wrong," Tavarian said. But he rolled off the bed and headed to his massive walk-in closet on the other side of the room.

I took a minute to enjoy the *very* fine view, then reluctantly dragged myself from the bed to wash and dress.

On our way to the formal dining room, a wave of alarm raced down the bond.

"*Zara!*" Lessie cried. "*Three airships are approaching!*"

"Shit!" I gave Tavarian the message, then bolted for the stairwell. "Warn the others!" I shouted at him.

He ran in the other direction as I raced up the stairs and out the nearest window. My hands nearly froze as they gripped the icy roof edge. With winter here, the weather on Tavarian's island was downright frigid, but I ignored it and hauled myself onto the roof.

Sure enough, a small flotilla of airships approached the island. "*Lessie,*" I started, but I didn't even have to finish my thought. The three dragons shot into the air, glittering red, gold, and blue in the late morning sunshine. They spread their wings wide as they lined up to face the ships, both to make themselves look more menacing and to form a barrier in case one of them decided to try and take a shot at the house with those cannons. My heart slammed against my rib cage as I gripped my dagger, feeling powerless. The ships were out of range, but if they got close enough...

But the ships seemed to decide that getting in range of dragon fire was not worth whatever damage they might take. Faster than I thought possible, they turned tail and raced away.

"Well, that was anticlimactic," Lessie said, sounding quite disappointed. "I was looking forward to taking down a few more of those."

I sighed. "I guess the Zallabarians have decided to make their move on the floating islands sooner than anticipated." I sincerely hoped they wouldn't come back with more ships—we could fight off a few, but three dragons were no match for an armada.

When I returned inside the house to discuss the situation with the others, they seemed relieved.

"Those ships weren't flying Zallabarian colors," Jallis pointed out. "It's quite possible they were from another country, coming to investigate."

"But why?" Rhia asked. "Who would dare invade our airspace like that and risk angering the Zallabarians?"

"There are many reasons," Tavarian said. "The neighboring countries will want to know the extent of the occupation and how many resources the Zallabarians are expending. A smart general with the right resources could see this as a time to strike, while Zallabar is spread too thin and has not yet mobilized the resources of the country it has conquered."

"That's just what we need," Jallis grumbled. "Another country trying to take our land."

The next few days remained tense as we made a slow circuit around the country, but we encountered no other airships as we traveled to the hidden estate. To our relief, the old couple who ran Tavarian's estate were alive and well, the estate itself untouched by the war. There was a very heartfelt goodbye between us and the orphanage staff and children, particularly on Mrs. Thomas's part. If not for both the orphanage's and Tavarian's staff assuring her they were sufficient to take care of the orphans, I wasn't sure she would have left them at all.

"Will you come back and see us?" one of the toddlers asked, pointing a chubby hand toward Lessie. "I want to ride a dragon again."

"You will," Mrs. Thomas said as she squeezed him tight. "When all of this is over, you will all ride dragons again."

"Should she be giving them false promises like that?" Jallis muttered from behind me. "For all we know, these children may never see a dragon again."

"It is far better to give them hope than despair," Tavarian said quietly as he watched the children hug Mrs. Thomas goodbye. "The responsibility to make sure that the right future comes to pass is on our shoulders, not theirs."

"*FINALLY,*" Lessie said as Polyba came into view. "*I never thought I'd say it, but I'm ridiculously glad to see this place again.*"

"*Me too.*" I was relieved we'd managed to make it back in time. With the extra load the dragons had to carry, we'd had to stop for rest breaks. The flight over the open ocean had worried me the most, with nowhere for the dragons to stop if they got tired, but Lessie and the others handled the journey like champs, their wings strong and true as they carried us across the sea.

Kade and the other council members were gathered in the courtyard as we landed, practically buzzing with excitement.

"Commandant!" he exclaimed as we dismounted. "Thank the skies you're back. We were worried something terrible had happened when you didn't return with the rest of the party."

"We ended up taking on a side mission," I said, clapping him on the shoulder. "Did everyone else make it back safely?"

"One of the teams hasn't made it back yet, and another suffered great losses," he said, his expression turning sober. "The village they were assigned to was better defended than we anticipated, and two out of the three dragons were shot down. The third officer barely made it back alive."

Kade's words slammed into my chest, a sucker punch of emotion that temporarily stunned me. "Is the officer who made it back unharmed?"

"He's all right," Kade said. "Grieving, but all right."

"We will hold a vigil for the ones we've lost," Tavarian said as he came up from behind me. "Tomorrow night. First, we have urgent business we must complete."

We unloaded the weapons and treasure from the dragons. Despite the loss of two more dragon rider pairs, the soldiers were overjoyed to see the spoils we'd brought back, and they quickly squirreled away the treasure in one of the tower rooms.

"This will be more than enough to buy the supplies we need," Daria said excitedly after she'd finished cataloguing everything. "Between everything the teams managed to retrieve, we've got enough to feed everyone here for years."

Treasure wasn't the only thing the other riders had brought back. There were six children playing in the great hall—boys and girls rescued from dragon rider families. Rhia's mother—who had been tempted to stay at the estate but had come with us after Rhia told her she would be needed—set on them immediately, fussing like a mother hen and scolding the hapless soldiers who had been assigned to them for not making sure the children were bathed and properly dressed.

"Maybe we should take them to the hidden estate to join the others," I said. "They might be safer there."

"Perhaps, but we don't have time," Tavarian said. "We need to leave for the forge soon, and it is too risky to send a team there without being able to cloak them. A Zallabarian ship could follow them to the estate."

"Right." I watched as Mrs. Thomas herded the children from the great hall, presumably to get them cleaned up. At least Rhia's mother was here to look after them, which took a great burden off my shoulders.

Now that all the treasure had been secured, I called a meeting with both the council members and the dragon rider teams who had returned. Captain Ragorin gave a quick report on the status of the base. They'd made a number of improvements, including repairing some of the outer walls and making the building more defensible, and the group was now ruthlessly organized and efficient.

"The airship is nearly repaired as well," he said proudly. "We should be able to do a test run next week."

"Has there been any activity from the other tribes?" Jallis asked.

Captain Ragorin shook his head. "The Porcillas family has kept their distance," he said. "Though one of our sentries did report seeing a few scouts earlier today."

Tavarian and I exchanged worried glances. "We're going to need to visit them first thing in the morning," he said grimly. "They've seen the dragons returning and must know we've made it back. If we do not call on them soon, they will think we've broken our word."

We went around the rest of the group, getting reports from each of the rider teams on how their missions went and what they retrieved. Aside from three teams—the one that had suffered casualties, along with one that had not returned and a third that found their target estate already looted and abandoned—the rest had successfully managed to bring back either children or eggs.

"Eight eggs and six children," Tavarian said proudly. "You've all done very well."

The dragon riders seemed to glow beneath Tavarian's praise. "We brought back treasure, too, but nothing like what you did," Kade said. "We're definitely going to need to do another run soon and try to hit the other floating estates before the Zallabarians get to them."

Tavarian nodded. "If we take the proper precautions, there is no reason not to," he said. "This stealth mission is proof that dragons are still valuable in warfare. Their ability to glide stealthily through the air at night is absolutely essential."

"But still not enough to take back the country," Captain Ragorin lamented. "We'll need more men, and better weapons, if we hope to accomplish that."

As the meeting continued, the talk turned to grim tidings. The other riders reported the same things Tavarian, Rhia, Jallis, and I witnessed in Zuar City: greedy citizens buying up dragon rider homes on the cheap and collaborating with the invaders. Plenty of citizens were resentful and angry toward the riders, who they felt had precipitated their suffering, but many were also angry at the Zallabarians.

"The first stirrings of revolt are already happening, though," Ullion said. "And I think the soldiers we've planted in the towns and villages aren't going to find it hard at all to fan those flames."

"Agreed," Rhia said, "but it will take some time for a rebellion to build up any steam. In the meantime, we need to do everything we can to make things difficult for the Zallabarians, including finding new allies, if possible. Perhaps whoever sent those ships to scout the floating islands might be someone we can team up with."

"We need to find out what's happened with the overseas colonies," Jallis said. "The Zallabarians probably haven't had time to hit them yet, so we might be able to form a new base that's less hostile."

"We should send an envoy to investigate," Tavarian agreed, "but we must be cautious. If the locals have found out that Elantia has fallen, they might very well decide to revolt against the government. Most of the colonies are very stable and prosperous, so there is little worry of that, but I've seen this thing happen far too often to not be wary. We will need to gather intelligence first, or at the very least some news."

"I can help you with that," Halldor said as he walked in. He was still wearing his dragon rider armor, his cheeks pink and his curly red hair windblown, and I didn't miss the way Rhia sat up straighter at his arrival. "I've got plenty of news from Warosia."

"Halldor!" I nearly jumped up to hug him before remembering there was a plate of food on my lap. "Did you bring the canvas back?"

"Sure did," he said with a grin as he took his seat between Rhia and Tavarian. His knee bumped against Rhia's, and I had to hide a grin of my own as she blushed. "Already dropped it off with the crew."

"You went to visit a friend of yours in Warosia, didn't you?" Rhia asked.

Halldor nodded, turning his attention to her. "Kal. He's well connected to the Warosian court, so I managed to finagle an audience with the king."

"King Rodici?" Tavarian was astonished. "He does not give audiences to just anyone. What did you say to him?"

"It's what he said to me that's important," Halldor said, his grin widening. "Turns out the king is getting pretty nervous about Zallabar. Apparently, they've got their sights set on Ruisin and Traggar next, and the Warosians don't want to wait around until Zallabar decides to go after them, too. They want to make an alliance with us, but only if Tavarian personally oversees the negotiations."

The others burst into excited chatter at this as Tavarian and I looked at each other. I could tell he was just as conflicted as me. On the one hand, this was an excellent opportunity. A lucky break, in fact, as there weren't that many potential allies on the continent to begin with. But we couldn't delay our trip to the forge any longer. I hoped to be on our way in the next forty-eight hours.

"The king said you will be treated as the representative for the Elantian government-in-exile," Halldor went on when everyone had quieted a little. "You are the only one left with the power to make these negotiations, as the rest of the original council has been taken prisoner. They fled to Winnia, but a group of insurgents had already deposed the governor by the time they got there."

"That is most unfortunate," Tavarian said, but the rest of the group did not share his sentiment, and neither did I.

"*Serves those bastards right,*" Lessie huffed. "*They deserve nothing less after abandoning us.*"

"Agreed." I squeezed Tavarian's hand, silently glad that he hadn't gone with them.

"There is also," Halldor added, a sly smile coming to his lips, "a mage at the Warosian court who is a scholar of ancient lore. She specializes in magical warcraft, so if anyone can help us figure out how to use that horn, it's her."

"It sounds like an opportunity I cannot afford to pass up," Tavarian said cautiously, "but the Warosians will not ally with us without expecting something in return. There will be a price to pay."

But the dragon riders didn't seem to care about that. All they knew is that we needed to get off this forsaken island, and that an alliance was our best bet for striking back at the Zallabarians.

After lunch, Tavarian and I gathered up the weapons we'd promised as payment and secured them in one of the litters. As we flew to the Porcillas settlement with three other riders in tow, we discussed our plans.

"I don't think that we can afford to keep the Warosians waiting," Tavarian said into my ear as the wind whipped around us. "If the king wants to make an alliance, we need to jump on that opportunity."

"I know." I sighed as I leaned into him. "And if that mage can help us figure out how to use the horn, all the better. But I don't like the idea of us separating, Tavarian."

"I don't either." He tightened his arms around me. "But perhaps there is a way for us to do both without having to go our separate ways."

"We'll discuss it later," I said as the settlement came into view. I tensed, half-expecting another volley of arrows. Although sentries stood on the rooftops, bows and arrows at the ready, they didn't fire. I heaved a sigh of relief as we made it to the chieftain's house. This time when we knocked, we were let in without hesitation.

"For you," I said as we laid the litter full of weapons on the floor in front of the chieftain's throne. "In exchange for the horn."

The chieftain's eyes shone greedily as he beheld the array of steel. "This is quite an offering," he said.

We actually had more weapons back at the base—we planned to offer these first, then a second half once we determined the horn worked—but judging by the chieftain's reaction, it looked like we wouldn't need it.

"The horn is yours," he said, snapping his fingers, and one of his wives, the fierce woman who'd tried to throw us out the last time we'd come here, came forward with the box. I could feel the power thrumming from the object within before I even took it, and when I touched the box I had to hold in a gasp as the power flowed up and down my skin.

"Let it be known that the blood debt has been paid," the chieftain said, thumping his staff on the floor. "So long as you honor our traditions and respect our property, we shall no longer attack you and yours."

"Thank you," Tavarian said. "The next time we meet, I hope it can be as friends."

The chieftain sent us on our way, but not before we promised to come back to trade the next time we got supplies from Warosia. We'd greatly impressed them with the weapons, and they were eager to see what else we could bring.

"Who knows," I joked as we flew away. "Maybe if we stay here long enough, we can turn Polyba into a thriving civilization."

Dismissing the other dragons, I asked Lessie to fly us to some remote cliffs overlooking the ocean, far away from any settlements. Sliding down from her back, I stood atop the rocky cliff and glanced around. "I think that should work as a good test target," I said, pointing to a large boulder sitting on an adjacent cliff about a hundred yards away. "I'm guessing you activate this thing by blowing into it?"

"Presumably, yes," Tavarian said. "But hang on a minute." He flicked his hand in a complicated gesture, summoning a glowing blue shield around us. "This should protect us from any shrapnel," he said.

My stomach knotted itself with anxiety as I lifted the horn to my lips, but I steeled myself for any impact and blew anyway. A deep, clear sound echoed from the horn, and everyone tensed, waiting for something to happen.

But nothing did. No magical energy issued forth from the mouth of the horn, or anything else. And the boulder stubbornly remained where it was.

"Damn." I tried again, but the same thing happened. "I guess this was a waste of time."

"Hmm." Tavarian took the horn from me, studying the runes carved into the bone. "I can't read these, but they do look somewhat familiar. Perhaps the mage in Warosia can help decipher them. I've no doubt these are instructions. Perhaps the horn must be prepared with certain herbs before it can be used, or there must be certain weather conditions."

I frowned. "That seems stupid, though," I said. "Why would you design an item that's so finicky if you intend to use it during wartime?" A thought occurred to me, and I nudged Tavarian. "Why don't you try it?"

"I doubt me blowing on it will make any difference," Tavarian said dubiously, but he lifted the horn to his lips anyway. The sound that issued from the horn sent a chill through me. It was ten times louder, reverberating through my bones as if I were sitting directly on a fault line. The air shimmered as an unseen force barreled toward the boulder, and a thunderclap rent the air as the magic struck true.

"Get down!" Tavarian yelled, yanking me to the ground as the boulder shattered into a million pieces. Even at this distance, deadly shards rained overhead, and I screamed as the cliffs shook uncontrollably. Loud crashes sounded all around us, as if the entire world was being shaken apart. My amulet flashed, pouring bright white light over us, but terror raced through me as I realized Lessie was unprotected.

"Lessie," I croaked, struggling to my feet. But a wave of nausea drove me back to the ground, and I vomited up the contents of my stomach. Tavarian and Lessie retched as well, a side effect of the magic and not just my nerves getting the better of me. My head felt like someone had clamped a vise around it, and something warm trickled from my ears and down the sides of my neck.

"Blood," Tavarian rasped. He reached out and dragged a finger along the side of my neck, and I was horrified to see it come away wet and glistening red. "Dragon's balls, what did that thing do to us?"

"Seems like we suffered the blowback," I managed, then closed my eyes and leaned my head against the ground. I was in too much pain to think further than that, never mind speak.

"This thing is dangerous," Lessie said, her voice vibrating with anger. She nudged me with her snout, and when I didn't move, curled her tail around me protectively. *"It didn't affect me*

the way it did you, but if I'd been flying when Tavarian had blown that thing we all would have fallen from the sky."

I wasn't sure how long we lay there, but flapping wings stirred me from the fetal position.

"Zara! Lord Tavarian!" Halldor cried as he jumped off his dragon and rushed toward us. He dropped to the ground beside me and rolled me onto my back. "Skies, what the bleeding hell happened to you all?"

"We tried using the horn," Tavarian croaked. He finally managed to get upright, pushing himself into a kneeling position so he could survey our surroundings. "Bloody hell," he muttered. "The cliffs."

Halldor helped me into a sitting position, and my mouth dropped open. The entire section of cliffs beneath the boulder had fallen away, and even a portion of the cliff we'd been standing on was gone.

"No wonder it felt like an earthquake," I said numbly as I gazed at the destruction. "We were standing in the middle of the cliff when Tavarian blew the horn. Now we're practically at the edge."

"Yeah, and on that note, let's get you away from the edge before more of the cliff decides to break off," Halldor said. With Lessie's help, he guided us to more solid ground, where Kiethara was waiting. "Are you guys well enough to ride?"

"Not quite," Tavarian said shakily. "I doubt Zara is either."

Halldor released me, and I tried to stand. But the nausea made me dizzy, and I had to crouch, sticking my head between my legs.

"Here." Tavarian helped me the rest of the way to the ground. "Let me heal you."

"Do you have the energy for that?" I asked as he placed his hands on either side of my head, but Tavarian didn't answer. Closing his eyes, he began murmuring under his breath. A warm glow enveloped my head, and I gasped as pain lanced through my skull. Lessie growled, sensing my suffering, but the pain quickly faded as the magic did its work, healing the ruptured and inflamed tissue and banishing the crippling nausea.

Tavarian was pale with strain when he released me, sweat dotting his brow. "I think you'll have to get me on the saddle yourself," he said, then tilted forward, his eyes already sliding shut.

"Tavarian!" I caught him as he slumped against my chest, then pressed my hand against the side of his neck, feeling his pulse. It was weak, but still there. "Dammit. Halldor, can you help me lash him to the saddle?"

The two of us lifted Tavarian onto Lessie's back and tied him to the front of the saddle so I could slide in behind him.

"Whatever this weapon is," Halldor said as I tucked the horn into one of my pouches, "it's obviously too dangerous to be used in its current form."

As we flew back to base, I tried not to dwell on things that could have gone much worse.

"*At least we know this thing works, right?*" I told Lessie as I lifted my face and the wind flowed through my hair. There was something so refreshing about that, as if the wind's fingers were dusting the cobwebs off my brain and clearing my head. "*And if*

Tavarian is able to meet with that Warosian mage, maybe she'll be able to teach him how to use it properly."

"I hope so," Lessie said. *"It's obvious that the horn was intended to be wielded by a mage, so with any luck, she will know how to minimize the blowback."*

Tavarian had regained consciousness by the time we landed in the courtyard, and he was able to walk, albeit assisted.

"Don't worry about me," he said as I helped him inside. "I should be all right after a good night's sleep."

We were just about to head upstairs to bed when Halldor grabbed my arm.

"Seven people are approaching at great speed," he said. "I think the missing team is back!"

Relief swept through me, banishing the lingering anxiety from our weapon experiment, and even Tavarian seemed to perk up.

"They must have managed to retrieve some of the children," he said as we headed back outside.

Rhia and Jallis joined us just as three dragons touched down. "Thank the skies," Jallis exclaimed as the riders dismounted. "What happened?"

"We ran into a bit of trouble trying to sneak these little ones out of their home," a female rider said as she helped a young boy off the dragon. He was blond and rosy-cheeked, his eyes big and round as he stared at us. My heart ached for him; he couldn't have been more than eight years old. "But they've been very brave," she added, ruffling the kid's head.

"Is there food?" a little girl asked plaintively as she was

helped down from another dragon. Four children in total. Rhia's mother was going to be thrilled. "I'm so hungry."

"Here, let's get you inside for a hot meal before bed," Rhia said with a smile. "I'm sure my mother would love to whip you up something to eat."

"Yay!" The children perked right up, rushing past Rhia to get inside. But as the blond boy passed her, a loud crack came from the pouch on Rhia's hip, and he jumped, startled.

"What was that?" he cried, turning to face Rhia. But a grin was already spreading across all of our faces, and as Rhia flipped open the flap on her pouch, the answer poked his head out.

"Looks like you're a dragon rider now, buddy," she said as the tiny dragonling squirmed out of the pouch. The little boy shrieked in delight as the dragon leaped at him, and he caught the tiny, wriggling beast in his arms. Its scales were gold dappled with green, reminding me of Kadryn, but in reverse. "I meant to put the egg away after we got back, but I felt like carrying it around a little longer. Guess my intuition must have been telling me you would arrive!"

"This is a cause for celebration!" Jallis exclaimed. "Come, let's get the two of you inside so you can clean him up and eat. Has your dragon told you his name yet?"

"Her," the little boy said proudly. "Her name is Minaxa."

"Would you look at that," Lessie said, her voice alight with glee. *"Finally, I'm no longer the youngest dragon around!"*

I laughed. *"Be careful,"* I warned as we went inside. *"I might just assign you as her dragon mom."*

"You know," Lessie said thoughtfully, *"I don't think I'd mind that at all."*

THIRTEEN

That night, Tavarian and I went to sleep in good spirits. The arrival of a baby dragon had lifted everyone's mood, and we'd celebrated with a nice big bonfire in the courtyard, dancing and singing and telling stories about the great dragon riders from our history. The fact that the dragonling was a female made her arrival even better. Female dragons had become very rare, and the procreation rates for dragons had been dropping steadily over the last century. If we could bring just a few more baby dragons into the world, we could get a head start on increasing the dragon population.

As I drifted off to sleep, I dreamt of a different world. A world where Elantia was free of Zallabarian rule and where dragons didn't have to fight anymore. Standing atop a plateau, I watched as six baby dragons scampered across the field, wrestling and chasing and play-fighting with one another. Lessie and a few other dragons stood watching nearby, their eyes shining with love and pride, and my own heart swelled as I realized at least one of the babies belonged to her.

"*Which one is yours?*" I asked as I walked over to lean against her bulk.

She nuzzled the top of my head briefly before turning back to watch the dragonlings. "*You can't guess?*" she teased.

My gaze immediately went to a dragonling the size of a large dog, with iridescent blue scales the same color as Lessie's. "*She's got green spikes instead of gold,*" I noted slyly. "*Is Kadryn the father?*"

Before Lessie could answer, a dark shadow passed over the sky. I shivered as the sun disappeared and a cold wind whipped through the air. Suddenly the dragons went still, even the babies, and an awful feeling took root in my heart as they all looked to the sky.

"My children." A deep, terrible voice echoed through the sky as the dark shadow spread across it. To my horror, it took the shape of a large, black dragon with glowing red eyes. "It is time to come home."

"No," I said, my voice trembling. The dragonlings screeched, flapping their wings furiously as they leaped through the air, but they were too young to fly yet. "No, you can't take them!"

But the other dragons took flight, and not just the ones standing near me. Others rose into the air from their perches on the cliffs and mountains surrounding us, joining the growing blight that spread across the sky. Only Lessie remained, but when I turned to her for an explanation, she didn't respond. She was staring at the sky, her eyes blank as if she was in a trance.

"*Lessie?*" I slapped her shoulder, trying to get her to respond.

But she said nothing, and the bond between us was a wall of blackness. No, not a wall, I realized with growing horror.

There was nothing there at all.

"Kill her," the evil voice commanded, and Lessie turned to me, maw opening wide as fire barreled up from her throat...

"Zara!"

I bolted upright at Lessie's voice.

"Zara, are you all right?" Lessie asked, her voice stretched taut as a wire. "I could sense your pain and fear."

The bond. I reached out for Lessie through the bond, and nearly cried in relief as her consciousness brushed against mine. "I had an awful dream," I said, pressing a hand against my galloping heart. My breathing was ragged. "I dreamed that Zakyiar turned all the dragons against us, and that he made you kill me."

Stunned silence greeted me at the other end of the bond. "You know that I could never harm you, Zara," Lessie finally said. "And even if I did, the bond would kill us both."

But I shook my head bitterly. "I don't think the dragon god would care about that," I said as Tavarian stirred beside me. "In fact, I think it would give him great pleasure to make us kill each other."

"It's never going to happen," Lessie said stubbornly. "I would sooner set myself on fire than harm a hair on your head."

"You're fireproof, Lessie," I said, a little irritably.

"You know what I mean," she growled. "Besides, Zakyiar is

just trying to terrify us into turning against each other. I was dreaming that a group of humans surrounded me and stabbed at me with pitchforks, screaming, 'DEATH TO THE DRAGONS!' We can't let him win, Zara."

"You're right." I let out a long, slow breath. "I'm sorry, Lessie. It's just so hard."

She gave me a mental hug through the bond, melting away the fear and terror that had hooked their claws into my soul.

"It's hard on us all," she said, "but undoubtedly the dragon god will hit you the hardest. We just have to be prepared for that and shrug it off as best as we can."

Tavarian's arms slid around my waist from behind, and I leaned into him, allowing him to take the burden of my weight. "You having bad dreams too?" he murmured.

I turned sideways so I could snuggle against his chest and told him about the dream. "I had a similar nightmare," Tavarian said as he stroked my back. "I was flying with Muza when suddenly the dragon god appeared in the sky and took control of him. He started torching villages and razing crops, eating any humans who tried to get in his way." He shuddered. "I tried to get him to stop, but it was as if the bond was severed. He wouldn't listen to me at all."

"Do you think that would really happen if the dragon god was resurrected?" I asked. "That he would sever our bonds and take control of all the dragons?"

"It's a real possibility," Tavarian said gravely. "But then again, the dragon god might just want to make us think that."

We drifted back to sleep again, but I awoke three more times with similar dreams—blood-soaked portents of the future should we fail. And when I stumbled down the stairs to the breakfast hall, I noticed that I wasn't the only one who was tired. Everyone else, even the non-rider soldiers, was pale and haunted, shadows dogging their eyes.

"Let me guess," I said as I sat down with Rhia, Jallis, and Halldor. "You've had bad dreams too?"

"Awful ones," Jallis said in a brittle voice. "I dreamed I was back at my family estate, having a meal with my parents, and Kadryn set our entire home on fire. I woke up just before we burned alive."

"I don't even want to talk about mine," Rhia said in a quiet voice. She chased a piece of potato around her plate with a fork but made no move to pick it up.

"What are these dreams?" Halldor demanded. "And why are we all having nightmares at the same time?"

"It's the dragon god," I said wearily. "He's trying to wear us down in our sleep."

Tavarian called the rest of the council members over to our section of the hall, and I explained the situation with the dragon god and our impending quest at the forge.

"I'm sorry this has affected you all," I said. "Now that we have two pieces of the heart in close proximity, the dragon god must be able to exert more influence. I'll set out for the forge right away so we can deal with this threat permanently."

"So, the dragon god is still alive?" Captain Ragorin said incredulously. "On another plane of existence?"

"Sort of," I said. "His soul is powerful enough that he's able to reach us from whatever world he's been cast into. I think it's because his heart was never actually destroyed. If the mages from the Dragon Wars had been able to get rid of it completely, then the dragon god wouldn't have any link to our world."

"I hate to see you leave already," Captain Ragorin said. "Is there no one else who can go?"

I shook my head. "The ancient gods have named me as their champion. I have to be the one."

"Ancient gods," Daria muttered. "Now I really have heard everything. You're not seriously thinking about going alone, are you, Zara? Because that would be madness."

I hesitated. "Rhia and Tavarian were supposed to come with me, but Tavarian needs to oversee the negotiations with Warosia. And I don't want to put anyone else in danger if I don't have to." I glanced furtively at Rhia.

Rhia crossed her arms and glared at me. "We've already been over this, Zara. I'm going with you."

"I wish I could come with you, especially since Tavarian can't," Jallis said heavily. "Maybe I could hand—"

"No," I said firmly. We'd already decided Jallis would lead the stealth missions, and between aiding the resistance and looting the remaining floating islands, there were still a number to carry out. "You're needed here."

"Then I'll come in his place," Halldor announced. "My ability to sense hidden enemies will come in handy, and besides, I want to see the old gods for myself." He clapped Rhia on the shoulder and grinned at her. "It'll be fun, won't it?"

"This is supposed to be a dangerous mission, Halldor," Rhia scolded, but she was blushing again.

"Maybe," he challenged, meeting my gaze, "but there's no point in charging into things with a doom-and-gloom attitude.

You were a treasure hunter before you became a rider, weren't you, Commandant? Don't tell me you didn't look at every expedition as an adventure."

A thousand arguments sprang to my lips about how this was nothing like an expedition, but they died. Halldor was right.

"You're damn right I did," I said, forcing a grin. I was born with a sense of adventure, if nothing else, and I wasn't going to let Zakyiar take that away from me, no matter how hard he tried.

FOURTEEN

"I hate that we have to do this," Tavarian said as we stood on the balcony together. We watched the sunset together after spending most of the day packing and preparing—him for his trip to Warosia, and me for my journey to the forge. "If I could, I would meet you at the forge when I'm finished with this negotiation."

"No." I laced my fingers in his as the sunlight shifted from gold to pink. *At least it's not blood red*, I thought, remembering my dreams from last night. With everything I'd seen and done, I wondered if red sunsets were omens, and the last thing I needed was a portent of doom to herald the beginning of my quest. "The others need you more. Besides, there's no reason to put yourself in danger."

"I would slay any monster, face down any god, to keep you safe," Tavarian said. He tilted my head back so that I looked up at him, his silver eyes brimming with emotion. "You have to know that by now, Zara."

"I do." My lower lip trembled, but I smiled anyway. "It's what I love about you. You serve your people selflessly, regardless of what they say or think about you. That's not something I would have been capable of before I met you. I was selfish and greedy, out for myself. Being with you has changed me."

"Greedy, maybe," Tavarian teased as he hooked a curl behind my ear. "But never selfish." He dipped his head, lips brushing mine, and the spark of need deep in my center ignited into full-blown desire. Sinking my hands into his silky black hair, I kissed him back for all I was worth until the two of us were panting and tearing at each other's clothes.

"Are you sure?" he asked as he lifted me up to sit on the balcony edge. The chilly breeze whipped around us, tugging at my hair, and I knew that if Tavarian let me go I would tumble off the edge to the rocky precipice below.

Yet there was something exciting about being on the brink like this. My shirt was open, my trousers were down around my ankles, and anyone could see us if they passed beneath the tower. I was standing on the knife's edge between life and death, and I'd never been more aroused.

"Yes," I growled, and yanked him against me. Our mouths met in a clash of teeth and tongues as he sank inside me, and we made love furiously against the backdrop of the dying sun. Waves of pleasure steadily built until they burst inside me, a fiery crescendo that sent me soaring higher than any dragon flight.

"I love you," Tavarian said raggedly, his face buried in my hair. We were sweaty and spent, still leaning against the balcony, but for once my head was clear. There were no dark thoughts of failure or nightmares clinging to my thoughts, only a warm sense of bliss and comfort. His hand grasped mine, and something cold and metallic slipped around my finger. "When you get back, we're getting married."

I lifted my hand to see a large sapphire glinting on my ring finger. "That's one way to propose," I said, laughing. "Where are we going to find a priest?"

He grinned. "If you can make it back from the god of death's domain in one piece, I daresay finding a priest will be a cakewalk."

I caught his face in my hands, tracing the angular lines and planes with my thumbs. "You be careful too," I told him, serious now. "You may not be going to visit a death god, but your mission will be dangerous too." It was very likely there would be Zallabarian assassins and agents waiting for him in Warosia, just as there had been in Traggar. Tavarian had nearly been assassinated twice that I knew of, and the Zallabarians would be even more eager to get at him now.

"I will," he promised.

We retreated to our tower room to clean up, and then I went down to the courtyard to meet the others. Lessie was already saddled up, as were Ykos and Kiethara, and the soldiers were loading our luggage into the saddle bags.

"Here." I handed Halldor a leather pouch identical to the one that hung from my hip. "Keep this on you at all times. We can't afford to lose it."

"A piece of the dragon heart, eh?" Halldor took it, a mixture of fascination and revulsion on his face as he tugged open the flap. His eyes widened at the sight—it looked like a huge, coarsely cut black diamond. "I would think this was just a giant jewel if I didn't feel the horrible energy coming off this thing," he muttered. "No wonder we're having such awful nightmares."

"Speaking of nightmares," Daria said from behind us. We turned around as she headed toward us with the rest of the council in tow. She was carrying a pouch of her own, and she handed us three small tins from inside it.

"This is a special tincture, passed down from my mother's side of the family," she said. "Just smear a little bit of it under your nose before you go to bed and you'll have a dreamless sleep. The only thing is that it makes waking up before morning extremely difficult, so I would suggest that you don't all take it on the same night."

"Thank you." The thought of being unable to wake up if the dragon god was able to visit my dreams anyway made my insides clench in terror, but I decided not to mention that. Daria meant well, after all, and it was worth a shot, wasn't it?

"You'll promise to keep our secret, won't you?" Rhia reconfirmed with them.

They nodded. "We won't tell anyone where you've gone," Kade said. There was always a possibility one of Salcombe's minions would come to the island, or that the Zallabarians would get here before Tavarian managed to negotiate asylum for the rest of us. "See you on the other side, Commandant."

The group saluted, and the three of us returned the gesture before mounting up.

"*Let's go,*" I said to Lessie as the last of the sunlight finally died. Hopefully with the pieces of heart far away, the rest of the base would be able to rest easy tonight.

FIFTEEN

The first leg of our flight took four hours across the open ocean. We headed to Movaria, a different continent entirely, located in the east. We had a few colonies in the northern part of the continent, but after hearing about what happened to the council who'd decided to take refuge at Winnia, we decided to stay away from those entirely.

"I wish you'd had a chance to rest more," I said to Lessie as we lounged by the campfire. We'd chosen a small, uninhabited island to rest on for the day. Unlike Polyba, this place was verdant, with lots of vegetation and animals, a good place for the dragons to hide while we rested. "You were hit pretty hard by the horn's blowback, too."

"Not as hard as you," Lessie said, "and besides, I don't need to rest between flights as long as I used to. I've gotten quite a bit stronger."

"You sure have," I said as I stroked her glittering scales. "Maybe that fish diet has been good for you."

Lessie snorted at my joke, and I laughed. Despite the dangers ahead, it felt good to be on the road, or in the skies, again. While it was nice to have breaks, I belonged outside in the wide world, traveling to new places and embarking on new adventures.

"And getting ourselves into trouble, of course," Lessie said with a grin, and I laughed again.

"You two look like you're having a nice time," Halldor said as he and Rhia walked into the clearing. They'd gone to gather more wood for the fire while I stayed behind to roast the mussels and shellfish we'd gathered along the shoreline. "Mmm, that smells delicious."

"They should be done right about now," I said. I nudged the mussels out of the fire with a stick and onto a waiting leaf to cool so we could crack them open. "You find anything of interest?"

Halldor shook his head. "There's no one else living here."

"Makes sense." I hadn't sensed anything of value on the island when we'd landed, and I doubted I'd find much with an in-depth search. I supposed it was too small to be anything other than a private retreat, and for whatever reason no one had claimed it yet.

The dragons, satisfied that we would be safe for a while, took flight to hunt for their own breakfast while we ate ours.

"So," Rhia said after she'd swallowed a mouthful of shellfish. "What exactly can we expect once we arrive at the forge? Did Caor tell you anything useful?"

"Not really," I said, a little grumpy as I thought of the messenger god. "He just said that Derynnis doesn't like visitors, and it's fifty-fifty as to whether or not he'll help us."

"That explains why the forge is so damned hard to reach," Halldor said as he stoked the fire. It was nice to be able to sit around one without fear. On this remote island, and in broad daylight, we didn't have to worry about attracting attention. "I'm not looking forward to the voyage."

"Do you know anything about Derynnis at all?" Rhia prompted. "You've studied a lot about the ancient gods, Zara. Surely you've read something about him."

"Yeah, a little." And nothing good, but Rhia and Halldor deserved to know as much as possible. "Derynnis doesn't have the best reputation. He was feared by everyone. His job is to judge those who pass into the afterlife and make sure those who did not get punished for their evil deeds in life don't escape their fate. He tends to express his anger via earthquakes and erupting volcanoes, and he has dominion over the fires under our feet."

"The fires under our feet?" Halldor exclaimed. "But there is no such thing."

"Actually," Rhia said, "there are scholars who theorize there is a river of lava flowing beneath the earth. That's why it spews out of volcanoes."

"Really?" Halldor's brow furrowed. "I just thought there was a pool sitting beneath the volcano and that it got agitated every once in a while. I've never actually seen a volcano explode," he admitted. "Elantia doesn't have any active ones."

"In any case," I said, not wanting to get pulled into a scientific discussion that I didn't have any answers for, "we need to be prepared for opposition when we arrive at the island. Hopefully Caor will tell us more when he next decides to grace us with his presence." I raised my voice and pointedly looked toward the sky in case he was listening, but naturally, I received no answer.

Rhia laughed. "I guess the gods don't like to come when called."

"Not only do they not come when called, they show up when they're not wanted," Lessie said snidely.

"Maybe a little less vitriol?" I suggested. *"We kind of need the gods on our side for this one."*

Lessie said nothing, but I could feel her animosity in the bond. Not that I could blame her. The gods had made no secret of their dislike for dragons, so it was only natural that she would hate them as well. For our collective sanity, we finished the rest of our meal in peace.

"Do you have any family still in Elantia?" I asked Halldor as we cleaned up after the meal. "Or did they manage to escape?"

"I checked on my family estate when we went to Elantia, and it seems like they've fled," Halldor said bitterly. "It's occupied by Zallabarians now. I can only hope they won't trash the place too much or sell off all our family heirlooms before we can take the country back."

"I'm sorry." Rhia placed a hand over his. "I know what that's like."

"Yeah." He nodded, lacing his fingers with hers. "Your mother was driven out of her home too, right? That's why she's at Polyba with the rest of our group?"

"She would have stayed in Zuar City if we hadn't come to rescue her," Rhia said. "I think she might have been fine hiding out with friends since she's not a dragon rider. But I think it's best that she's away from it all, and the painful memories."

"Are your parents the only members left of your family?" I asked Halldor.

"There are others scattered around Elantia, but we were the only ones at the estate. My aunt, my father's younger sister, lived with us when I was little, but she left after she had a falling out with my father." His smile turned sad. "Actually, you remind me a bit of her, Zara. She had a very adventurous spirit and always wanted to travel to new places, or so my father said. And not to mention that red hair," he said, twirling a finger around his own curls. "Though we have that in common, too."

"I've never actually met someone with hair that looked so similar to mine," I said. I'd met people with red hair, and curly hair, but the combination itself seemed to be rare. "Does it run in your family?"

Halldor nodded. "Everyone from my father's side of the family has it."

My heart beat a little faster as pieces fell into place. "How long ago did your aunt leave? And how old is she?"

"Maybe thirty years ago?" Halldor scrunched up his face as he tried to remember. He would have been no more than five years old, so he couldn't have remembered her that well. "We never heard from her again, and I think my parents received news some years later that she had died." His gaze sharpened. "Why do you want to know?"

"Because," I said, not wanting to beat around the bush, "I think we might be related." I showed him my dragon blade and told him what little I knew. "There's a town in southwest Elantia I've been wanting to visit that may have answers," I told him. "Marcine."

"That's where my family estate is!" Halldor exclaimed. He scrutinized my face, inching closer to me. "I wish I remembered her face better. But you and I do share the same nose, I think."

"You do, now that I look at the both of you," Rhia said, sounding a little stunned. "The same chin, too. I'm not sure why I didn't see it before."

"There have been more important things to worry about," I said, a little breathless with excitement. "If I'm right, we might be cousins. What was your aunt's name?"

"Allara," he said. "Allara Savin."

"Savin." I tested the name out on my tongue. Of course, that wouldn't have been *my* family name, but it was close, closer than I'd been in a long time. "You know, there is one way to settle this for sure," I said, standing up.

Halldor eyed me apprehensively as I picked up my dragon blade. "And what way is that?"

Smiling, I handed him the weapon. "Take it for a spin. If you're able to wield it, that means you and I share a bloodline."

Halldor grasped the weapon, then gave it an experimental spin. I'd retracted the blades so that only the tips protruded from the handle, but when Halldor pivoted to the left and jabbed, the foremost blade shot out, extending to its full-length."

"Whoa." A delighted grin spread across his face. "I've heard of these blades before, but I'd never had a chance to try one out before! Where did you get it?"

"Jallis gave it to me," I said. "His family had it in their armory, but since I was able to use it, it obviously didn't belong to them. Since you can use it too, that means it must have originally been in your family."

"*Our* family," Halldor corrected. His grin softened as he handed the weapon back to me, the blades retracted once more. "Do you think we're cousins, then?"

"Most likely." I returned the blade to its sheath, then sat down heavily, my thoughts whirling in my head. Halldor, my cousin! Excitement raced through my veins at this new development—I was talking to a living, breathing member of my family! "When all this is over, I'd like to seek out your father and ask him some questions." This woman, Allara, might very well be my mother. Could it be the estrangement Halldor was talking about was over my father? Had he been a common ground-dweller, unsuitable for Allara in her brother's eyes? Or was there a feud between the families that had driven her away? The possibilities were endless.

The three of us discussed the issue for another hour before finally turning in. I decided against the tincture today, but even so I fell into a deep, relatively peaceful sleep. The three of us took turns watching while the dragons slept straight through—they needed the most rest since they were flying—but neither the dragon god nor anyone else disturbed us. I wondered if the dragon god could only attack us in our sleep in the night, or if he was busy elsewhere. And what of Salcombe? Was he tracking us across the sea, even now?

We awoke at twilight, and after a quick meal from the rations we'd brought with us, set off again. As we climbed higher and higher into the sky, a group of ships passed by, flying black flags from their masts.

"Pirates," Halldor said in disgust, his voice clear as a bell through our earpieces. "They infest the northern shores of the

Movarian continent, hitting coastal towns and dragging away both treasure and people to sell into slavery."

"Slavery?" Rhia sounded shocked. "Is that legal in this part of the world?"

"No, but that doesn't stop it from happening," Halldor said. "Rich, powerful men love to buy slaves, especially pretty women."

"We should set their sails on fire," Lessie growled, her anger sizzling through the bond. Kiethara tossed her head in agreement, smoke steaming from her nostrils, and I knew that if I gave the word, the three of them would gleefully dive-bomb the pirates.

"That's a nice idea, but what about the innocents who might be on board?" I countered. *"We would end up killing them too. Besides, the last thing we want to do is draw attention."*

Lessie drew in a longsuffering breath. *"Just once, it would be nice to throw logic aside,"* she said. But to my relief, she didn't try to challenge me, and neither did the other dragons.

Even so, I was tempted as we flew over the flotilla. The men on board craned their necks to watch us, many pointing and shouting in fear and awe.

"Zara, look! To the left!"

My heart leapt into my throat. A boy was arrowing through the water, heading straight for the island we'd just left. I zoomed in with my goggles. He couldn't be more than twelve, his scrawny body battling against the ocean waves as they tried to batter him back toward the ship. He must have taken the opportunity to escape, knowing his captors would be distracted by us.

"Dammit," I swore under my breath. We couldn't leave him there—he would drown. Taking my unspoken permission, Lessie dove for the waves. Gunfire exploded through the air as the pirates fired at us, and I sucked in a sharp breath as a cannonball hit the water only five feet from the boy. He sputtered as the resulting wave crashed over him, then shrieked as Lessie caught him up in her claws and shot back into the sky.

"Let me go!" he cried in Warosian, and I nearly fell off Lessie in shock. So he wasn't even from this continent? I leaned over the side to get a look at him, and gritted my teeth as he continued to fight, kicking and waving his arms about as he tried to get Lessie to dislodge him.

"Shut up!" Halldor snapped as Kiethara brought him level with the boy. "Do you want Lessie to drop you? You'll die from this height."

"What do you want from me?" The boy's voice was pitched high with fear. "I just escaped from one slaver. I'm not going to be taken by another!"

"We're Elantians, you idiot," Halldor said, his eyes flashing with impatience. "We don't practice slavery. Weren't the dragons a clue?"

"We're not here to hurt you," Rhia said gently. "We just saw that you were in trouble, and we wanted to help."

The boy stopped struggling, his lanky body sagging in Lessie's arms.

"Do you think I could sit with one of you?" he asked in a small voice. "It's a little uncomfortable, hanging here like this."

"*Ungrateful brat,*" Lessie huffed. But she deposited the boy on the back of Halldor's dragon, and Halldor secured him on the saddle in front of him.

Lessie pulled close enough to Kiethara that I could talk to the boy directly.

"I'm Zara, and this is my dragon, Lessie. We saw you in the ocean, and Lessie was worried you would drown, so she rescued you."

The boy's eyes narrowed. "How do you know that? Can she talk to you?"

"Yes. We have a telepathic link."

"Really? Can she talk to me, too?"

"Just me, unfortunately." I gave him a crooked smile. "But trust me when I say she has a mind of her own. She was trying to convince me to set those ships on fire right before we rescued you."

"I wish you had." A dark cloud passed over the boy's face. "The things they do to us...it would have been better to die, even in a fire, than continue to be a slave."

My heart ached at the raw pain in his voice, and if he'd been sitting on Lessie I would have been tempted to wrap him up in my arms and hug him. "I'm sorry you've suffered so much," I said gravely. "What is your name? And how did you get all the way out here?"

The boy's eyes filled with tears, and his lower lip trembled, just for a moment. "My name is Tibo," he said. "My parents and I were from Teluva." My brain instantly placed the town on a mental map—it was a coastal town in southern Warosia. "We'd heard the Movarian pirates were attacking nearby countries, but we didn't think they'd come to Warosia until two weeks ago when they attacked. My parents hid me in the cellar, but the pirates found me anyway." He sniffled, wiping at the tears running down his cheeks, but anger flared in his deep blue eyes. "I guess they thought I was pretty, because they decided to take me along instead of kill me."

A sick feeling settled in my stomach as I looked at Tibo again. Beneath the bruises and dirt on his face he was a handsome boy. That rat's nest of dark hair probably curled handsomely around his angular face, and he'd probably gotten his mother to give him anything he wanted with one look from those sapphire eyes. The look of horror on Halldor's face told me he was thinking the same thing I was—the boy would have met a terrible fate if he'd stayed on that ship.

"Do you know if your parents survived?" I asked cautiously. "Or were they taken with you?"

Tibo shook his head. "They were killed," he whispered. "I heard the pirates gun them down in the living room while I hid below. I wish..." His voice choked with tears. "I wish I'd been brave enough to do something. To fight them."

"There was nothing you could have done," Halldor said roughly. His annoyance had long vanished, and he gave the boy a one-armed hug. "You did exactly as your parents wanted, and you're here with us now. We'll get you someplace safe."

But where? I wondered as we flew into the night. The stars glittered coldly around us, like a sea of sharp diamonds ready to slice into us if we strayed off course. I didn't dare bring him along with us to the forge. The journey would be dangerous, and the forge was no place for a child. And we couldn't turn back to Warosia. We would lose too much precious time.

"We'll figure something out," Lessie said softly. *"We always do."*

"Yes." And despite the problem literally sitting in our laps, I couldn't regret saving the boy. After all, if we turned our backs on someone as badly in need as Tibo, we would be no better than the monsters we sought to destroy.

SIXTEEN

We flew until the sky turned light gray, signaling the coming dawn. Tibo was fast asleep in Halldor's arms when we landed in the ruins of an ancient pre-Dragon War settlement. It was a good twenty miles inland from the shore, and far enough from the closest town that we were relatively safe from pirates and prying eyes.

"This place is a little creepy," Halldor said as we made camp in one of the more intact buildings. Three of the ivy-covered walls were still standing, and part of the roof was even intact, though there was still enough of it exposed that it wouldn't keep any rain off us. "I think ghosts probably rise up from the ground at night and walk around the town, lamenting their lost lives and cursing whoever sacked this place all those years ago."

"Do you really think so?" Tibo asked, his eyes wide as saucers. He was already sitting on his bedroll, halfway through the hard biscuit I'd given him.

Rhia smacked Halldor on the shoulder. "Don't tell silly stories like that! You'll scare the boy."

Halldor laughed good-naturedly as he ruffled Tibo's hair. "There probably aren't any ghosts around," he admitted. "And even if there were, they won't come out during the daylight. Everybody knows that."

"So." I sat down on the ground and fixed Tibo with a stare. "Where do you want us to take you? Do you have any family on the continent here, maybe?" I hoped he did, since we couldn't afford to turn back.

Tibo shook his head. "Not that I know of, and my parents were the only family I had in Warosia." His face fell again, and he blinked rapidly to hold back tears. "I'm all alone now," he whispered.

"You're not alone," Halldor said, looping his arm around the kid's shoulder. "You've got us, and we're going to get you someplace safe."

"I think our best bet is to find a ship heading back to Warosia," Rhia said. "There are Warosian and Elantian ships that regularly make the crossing. Hell, even a Zallabarian ship would do, though of course we'd have to keep the dragons out of sight."

"What if I stayed with you?" Tibo asked hopefully. "I could work as your servant. My mother taught me a little bit about how to cook, and I can clean up after all of you. Maybe even take care of your dragon tack, too." He glanced through the missing wall at Ykos, who slept right outside. Lessie and Kiethara were off hunting while he guarded us.

"I wish I could take you on, but we can't afford it," I said.

"We're on a very dangerous mission. No offense, but we can't put you in danger by bringing you with us."

Tibo's shoulders sagged. "But what if the ship you put me on sells slaves?" he asked. "I've heard that some of the merchant ships smuggle slaves."

"We'll make sure to find a reputable captain," Halldor promised. "Someone who will take you on as a crew member. You can be a cabin boy for starters, perhaps, or they'll teach you how to be a proper sailor."

Tibo propped his chin on his fist, his brow scrunching as he gave the thought serious consideration. "I've always thought it would be cool to be a captain one day," he finally said. "If you can get me honest work aboard a ship, maybe I can rise up in the ranks when I'm older."

"That's the spirit." Halldor ruffled his hair as he gave the boy a fond smile. "Now let's get to sleep."

We bedded down for the night, and I took the first watch, sitting atop the wall as I looked out at the grassy landscape. The verdant landscape reminded me of Elantia, except there were no hills or mountains, and the forests were very far away. With my goggles, I could see deer grazing, and patches of grass waving here and there as smaller animals scampered underfoot. It seemed like a peaceful place, but I couldn't quite relax. Without any mountains or trees to shield us, I felt too exposed.

"I wonder if there was a river that cut through here once," Lessie said sleepily. *"Or maybe a lake. These people couldn't have survived without a water source somewhere."*

"Whatever it was, it dried up thousands of years ago." And had been ransacked long ago, I added privately. My treasure sense only picked up a few items buried in the ground—ancient artifacts that would fetch a high price, if I had the time to dig them up and sell them.

When it was Rhia's turn to take watch, I snuggled into my bedroll and fell asleep. At first, I thought the sunlight still kept the dragon god away, because I slept deeply for a while, a blanket of nothingness cushioning my mind. But that darkness gradually lightened until I was walking the city streets of Elantia again. The familiar glow of gas lamps surrounded me, illuminating the brick path I trod, but the crackle of the flames was the only sound. There was no laughter, no music, not even the whisper of a breath.

"That's because this city has abandoned you, Zara." Salcombe's voice echoed all around me, and I spun in a circle, trying to see where it came from. "How can you expect to return to it and find it as it once was?"

"Come out and face me, asshole!" I shouted. My voice bounced off the walls, and the buildings seemed to close around me, suffocating me, until I was being pressed between two slabs of concrete. No, not two slabs. I realized, as the world tilted, I was on one slab of cold metal that seared my naked flesh.

"Let me up!" I cried, pulling at my restraints. Hard leather banded around my wrists and ankles, pinning me to the table. But with each motion I made, an invisible blade slashed at my skin, until rivulets of blood were running all over my body.

"The more you struggle, the more it will hurt." Salcombe stepped from the shadows, except it wasn't Salcombe at all. His eyes were a pure, demonic red, and his skin was too white, too perfect, as if he were dead flesh made whole again. "Or at least that's what they all say, isn't it?" His grin widened, and I nearly screamed at the sight of long, sharp fangs protruding from his upper teeth. "The truth is I have no intention of sparing you, little champion. That reprieve I gave you last night was only meant to lull you into a false sense of security. To give you false hope that would make your pain all the sweeter when I invaded your fragile mind again."

He lifted his hands, and white-hot pain ripped through my body. "As long as you hold my heart, there is no escape," the dragon god snarled, his dark magic twisting inside me, tearing at my guts until I was a bloody, bleeding, writhing mass of pain. "I will tear you apart, piece by piece, until there is nothing left for your lover to hold. Until you can't even recognize yourself."

"Like hell you will!" I fought harder, pushing back with all the will I could muster. Hands clamped my shoulders, shaking me, and I lashed out with the only appendage left to me—my head.

"Oww!" Halldor's voice ripped through the air, jerking me from the dream. My eyes flew open as he fell back, rubbing the spot on his forehead where I'd struck him. "Dammit, Zara, that hurt!"

He was whispering in broad daylight, so I sat up, alert and ready. "What is it?" I whispered back. Rhia stood at the entrance, sword drawn. "Is someone coming?"

"Ten someones," Halldor said darkly. "They wear green paint and clothing that helps them blend in with the surroundings, and several of them carry scalps and shrunken heads from their belts. If not for my talent, I wouldn't have been able to spot them skulking in the grass." His jaw tightened as he helped me to my feet. "We've got maybe ten minutes until they're on us."

Scalps. Then these weren't the kind of men we could negotiate with. I nodded at Halldor, reaching for Lessie through the bond. *"Don't use fire,"* I warned her. *"We don't want to leave any trace that there were dragons here if we can help it."*

"Understood."

Rhia gave Tibo a dagger and ordered him to stay hidden while we crept out of the building. I extended my dragon blade halfway as I pressed against a crumbling wall closer to the north entrance of the town. I poked my head out just far enough to see the men entering the village. As Halldor had said, they were dressed entirely in green, their skin covered in some kind of tribal paint. To my relief, I saw that they carried no guns, only spears and bows and war axes. They spoke in a guttural language I didn't recognize, their eyes gleaming with undisguised bloodlust.

Ykos roared as he leapt over the building he'd been hiding behind in a single bound, snapping his wings out in the air. The men yelped in terror as he snatched one out of the air and crushed him between his talons, then swiped at the rest with his tail. They went down like a row of empty wine bottles, weapons clattering to the floor.

Rhia, Jallis, and I rushed them, yelling war cries as we went. Three of the men were on their feet by the time we reached them, and I gored one while Rhia slashed at another with her sword. Halldor spun through the others like a dervish with his twin blades, slicing them up like cows at a slaughterhouse. By the time we finished, blood spattered our armor and the nearby houses, running through ancient streets that probably hadn't seen this kind of action in centuries.

"Skies." Rhia wiped her blade off on one of the dead men's trousers before sheathing it. She looked a little pale beneath the spatter of blood that dotted her cheek. Though she'd seen warfare, she likely hadn't killed very many people in her short military career. "I think I'm going to be sick."

She spun around and made it ten feet before she collapsed to her knees and vomited. Halldor was beside her in an instant, holding her hair out of the way while she heaved her breakfast.

"It's all right," he said as she retched, rubbing her back in soothing circles. "You've got nothing to be ashamed of. It happens to everybody."

I retreated to our camp to check on Tibo and give Rhia and Halldor a bit of privacy. Part of me was glad I wasn't retching with her, but the rest of me wondered if I hadn't lost something of myself. But no, my retching days at the sight of dead bodies were long over. I'd killed far too many, both in the name of self-defense and in the defense of others, for blood and gore to turn my stomach now.

"Are they all dead?" Tibo asked when I walked in. He was clutching the dagger Rhia had given him, and his keen eyes took in my blood-covered armor with an intensity that was unsettling. "You didn't get hurt, did you?"

"No." I shook my head as I sat down behind him, reaching for a bottle of water and a rag to wash the blood off me. "With our dragons, they were no match for us."

"Good." He leaned his head back on the wall, his white-knuckled grip on the dagger finally loosening. "Don't feel bad," he said, glancing at me. "They deserved it."

I arched an eyebrow at him. "How do you know I feel bad?"

He shrugged. "You've got this look in your eyes that adults get when they're not sure they did the right thing." A sad look passed across his little face. "My mother would get that look sometimes when she punished me for doing bad things. But those men would have done worse if you'd let them live. If someone had taken down the men who attacked my village the way you killed these men, they'd be called a hero."

"Out of the mouths of babes," Lessie said, a little disbelievingly. *"You know, I'm glad we rescued this kid. I like him a lot."*

I smiled at Tibo. "You know, you're a pretty smart kid," I said. "Wherever you end up, I think you're going to do just fine."

SEVENTEEN

The next several days of flying were some of the most grueling traveling I'd ever done. With the dragon god determined to thwart us, our days were haunted by nightmares, making the night flights exhausting. We had to use the tincture Daria had given us, but one of us had to refrain each day, which meant we were still all short of sleep.

Worse, the tincture didn't work on the dragons at all, which meant they were feeling the strain worse than the rest of us. More often than not, we were woken by the dragons thrashing or roaring in their sleep. Once, Ykos had set fire to the field we'd been sleeping in. If Halldor, who'd been keeping watch, hadn't roused us from our sleep-in time, we might have lost our belongings in the resulting firestorm.

"At least we're not flying through the desert anymore," Lessie said on the fourth day. "I was worried that we would never see water again."

"Yeah, that was pretty nerve-wracking." Because the dragons

were so tired from lack of sleep, it had taken us three days to cross the vast Aranean Desert instead of one. Prior to that, we'd been flying over a tropical landscape thick with humidity, the forests crawling with all manner of poisonous and deadly creatures. But the desert had been worse. With only cacti and other strange desert plants, there had been no trees to shelter us from the sun as it pounded overhead. If not for the canvas tents we'd packed, I'm not sure we would have survived it at all.

Now we were finally flying through a temperate climate again, the country of Temeire sprawled beneath us. A large triangle, it made up the southernmost tip of the continent, surrounded on two sides by the vast Nirean Sea. My heart rose at the sight of ships traveling to and from the various port cities lining the coast. None were quite big enough to carry three dragons, but I was sure we would eventually find something.

"Let's land there," Halldor said, pointing to a thickly wooded region several miles inland. "That's only a few hours' journey to Roccar. If any captain has a ship large enough to transport all of us, we'll find it there—it's the largest port city in Temeire."

"Okay." We directed the dragons to land in the forest, settling in a clearing large enough for them to hide in. "You up for walking?" I asked Tibo as he slid off Ykos's back. He'd taken turns riding with each of us so as not to overtax the already exhausted dragons.

Tibo nodded, but the dark circles under his eyes worried me. "I can manage," he said stubbornly, lifting his chin as he caught the sympathy in my gaze. "I'm just as strong as you."

"No doubt about it, kid," Halldor said as he caught Tibo by the waist. The boy protested as Halldor lifted him onto his broad shoulders. "But you need your strength for tomorrow. Gotta be sharp for those interviews, right?"

Tibo nodded, his face tightening with nerves. We'd stopped twice on our journey in small villages, partly to refill our supplies, but also to see if there was a family who could take Tibo in. No luck so far, and though I'd never tell Tibo, I was starting to worry. What if we couldn't find someone to take him? Were we really going to bring him to the forge?

"Who knows," Lessie said wryly. "He might end up being helpful. For all we know, Derynnis has a soft spot for children."

"Not likely." I smacked her shoulder. "Now settle down and get some sleep."

The four of us took only the basic essentials, leaving the rest of our luggage with the dragons. They would stay tucked away in the forest while we scouted out the city, then meet us once we'd secured a ship. Though the piece of heart weighed heavily in the pouch on my hip with every step I took, I was happy that Halldor and I were taking the relics away from the dragons. Hopefully with some distance between us, the dragons would be able to get some good sleep for once.

By the time we arrived in Roccar, it was well after midnight, and Tibo was sound asleep in Halldor's arms. Luckily, we found an inn with a room large enough to accommodate all of us, and after taking first watch—no way would we let our guard down with two of the relics in our possession—I smeared some tincture under my nose, fell face-first into the bed, and instantly sank into a heavy, dreamless sleep.

THE NEXT MORNING, Halldor and I slipped out into the city while Rhia and Tibo slept.

"They're going to be pissed we left them behind," Halldor said cheerfully as we walked through the busy streets. "This place is fascinating."

"I agree."

As the largest port city in Temeire, Roccar was a bustling hive of activity. Conversations in more languages than I could count swirled around us as people from all over the world moved through the city, some in a hurry to their destination, others on leisurely strolls. The citizens seemed to come from all over the continent judging by their looks. Some had eyes the size of saucers, others narrow and slanted. There were bronze-skinned women with golden eyes, and pale skinned men with silver hair. Large, hulking brutes that looked like they crushed skulls for a living, and tiny waifs who were full grown and yet came up no higher than my waist. I'd never seen so much variety in one place before.

"But the nightmares seem to be hitting Rhia especially hard," I continued, "even with the tincture. I think giving her time away from the relics will help." As for Tibo, he was a growing boy who'd been through a lot of hardship. Giving him a soft bed to sleep on for as long as he wanted seemed like the least I could do.

"Yeah." Halldor sobered a little. "She's been incredibly strong through all this. I don't know that I would have been able to shoulder the amount of responsibility she has when I was her age."

I glanced sideways at Halldor. He was a few years older

than me—maybe thirty-two, thirty-three—while Rhia, though I often forgot it, was just coming up on twenty.

"Just how long have you had designs on Rhia?" I asked, remembering that he and Rhia had been at the same camp while I'd been stuck at the Traggaran Channel.

He smiled crookedly. "Since the moment I saw her," he said. "When she first walked into camp, she was nervous. She's gentler, more feminine, than the other female soldiers in the camp, and I think some people underestimated her in the beginning. But behind the fear I saw the steel, and I knew that with just a little bit of hammering, she'd become a formidable weapon."

I raised an eyebrow. "Exactly what kind of hammering are we talking about?"

Halldor's cheeks turned bright red. "That's not what I mean, and you know it," he sputtered as I cackled with glee.

"I know." I clapped him on the shoulder. "And that's why I'm going to let you marry her."

"Marry her?" Halldor looked like his eyes were going to bulge out of his skull.

"We can pick out a ring right now, if you'd like." I gestured to a ruby as we passed a jeweler's stall. "I think she'd like this one, don't you?"

Halldor let out an exasperated huff. "Quit messing with me."

I whirled around and poked him in the chest. "I will," I said, looking up into a pair of bewildered blue eyes that were far too similar to my own to be a coincidence. "Just so long as you understand that if you mess with her, you have to answer to me."

Halldor's gaze hardened. "Women's hearts aren't playthings," he growled. "I would never promise Rhia anything I wasn't prepared to follow through on."

"Good," I said cheerfully. "Then we understand each other."

I dropped my hand and continued walking, Halldor behind me muttering something about women. If it had been anyone else, I wouldn't have pushed, but I knew from my time spent with Rhia at the academy that she hadn't had much time for romance. When she wasn't training to be a dragon rider, she'd spent all her spare time helping her mother with the family shipping business. And because Rhia's family were of the merchant class despite being dragon riders, most of the guys, who came from noble families, hadn't been allowed to show interest in her. Now that one was, I needed to make sure that he wasn't going to treat Rhia like a conquest, someone to tumble in the hay with before moving onto bigger and better things.

She deserved better than that for her first time.

"Here we are," I said as we emerged from a shopping district. The port spread out before us, a long row of docks jutting out into the ocean. Dozens of vessels floated in the bay, at least ten large enough to carry dragons. "There's got to be someone here who will take us." We'd brought more than enough gold to buy off even the most recalcitrant captain.

"Yeah, if we can talk to someone who will understand a word we're saying," Halldor pointed out. We'd stopped by a food cart for breakfast, and the man who'd helped us had spoken no Elantian at all. "We might need to find an interpreter."

We walked the length of the docks, searching for someone who spoke a language we knew. Most of the merchants who owned shops here only spoke basic Elantian, and hardly any spoke Warosian or Zallabarian, but as we ducked into a small shop—really a shack—that specialized in net-mending, I was relieved to see an Elantian behind the counter.

"It's so nice to see someone from my home country," the man, who was called Aelor, said effusively once we'd stepped up to the counter and explained what we were looking for. "Do you have any news for me? I've heard some strange rumors."

"That our country has been taken by Zallabar?" I said. "Unfortunately, those rumors are true."

"Almost all the dragon riders have either fled or been executed, and the enemy now rules from Zuar City," Halldor added as the blood from the man's face drained.

"I... I thought..." He shook his head vigorously, as if trying to snap himself out of a great shock. "This is terrible news. I have family in southern Elantia. My sister and her family run a farm there. Do you think she's all right?"

"Unless she's got dragon rider blood or is a sympathizer, she's probably fine," I assured him, feeling guilty for making the man worry. After all, he was just a simple net-mender. What could he do about it? "I'm guessing you're a former sailor who left home to see the big, wide world?"

He gave me a half-smile. "I was. Sailed the seas for thirty years before I met my wife here in Roccar. We have two children now, so she's forced me to settle down, but every once in a while, I do feel the sea's call still." He glanced wistfully at the bay, visible through the small window at the front of the shop, but his eyes sharpened as he turned back to us. "Now, what can I help you with? I'm guessing you're refugees here to start a new life. Are you planning to take up fishing? I do sell nets as well as mend them," he said, gesturing to the netting displayed on the wall to our right. "But the industry is very competitive here, as I'm sure you know."

"We're actually looking to hire a ship," I told him. "There's a large island to the south of here that our group is trying to reach, and we have a lot of cargo." I explained what we needed in more detail, leaving out all mention of dragons and relics. "Do you think we could hire you as an interpreter?"

The man hesitated. "I don't know," he said. "My wife's not well today, and I can't afford to leave the shop—"

I placed a stack of coins on the counter. "Would this be enough?"

Aelor's eyes nearly fell out of his head, and I had to hide a smirk. I doubted he'd ever seen that much money pass over his counter in a single day, judging by the quality of his clothes and the size of his shop. "Umm, yes," he managed, hastily shoving the gold into his hands. "I think that should be more than sufficient. Let me lock up."

Aelor closed up shop, then led us away from the docks. "It's too much work to go to each of the ships individually," he explained as we passed a row of shops and restaurants. "If you want to hire a ship, you go to the Fat Mermaid. That's where all the captains go to arrange their cargo."

The man took us into a large tavern, which, aptly, did have a large, overweight mermaid poised above the double-door entrance. We went up to the bar, surprisingly crowded considering it was barely mid-morning. Halldor and I ordered the local drink, which was similar to mead but smelled spicy. I took a swallow and nearly choked when it raced down my throat, burning like wildfire.

"Dra—" Halldor started to swear, and then hastily changed the phrase. "Hell's fire," he sputtered, wiping his mouth with the back of his hand. "That's too strong to drink before lunch."

Aelor laughed, clapping him on the back. "It'll put some hair on your chest." He winked, and then led us over to the hearth, where a group of men were sitting.

"Captain Nemas," he said, addressing a handsome, broad-shouldered man in a captain's uniform. "These two are looking to hire a ship." He explained the size of our cargo and our price range.

"Pleasure to meet you." The captain shook my hand, the gleam in his eyes telling me that the amount offered definitely enticed him. "Can you tell me more about where you're headed?"

I hesitated, then lowered my voice. "The place doesn't have a name that I'm aware of," I said, "but it is a large, volcanic island, about two weeks' journey south of here. Do you know where I speak of?"

"The Hellmouth?" The captain reared back as if I'd struck him, his face turning ruddy. "I'm sorry, Miss, but you're out of your mind! Nobody travels to that cursed place."

"The Hellmouth?" Halldor asked eagerly, jumping into the conversation. "Is that its official name? What do you know about the place, Sir?"

"Any place that wretched must be the gateway to hell," the captain growled, "so that's what the locals call it. Nobody who sets out for that voyage ever returns alive. There is no amount of money you could offer to put my ship and crew at risk like that. I'm sorry, but you're just going to have to find someone else."

"You really want to go to the Hellmouth?" Aelor asked incredulously as the captain beat a hasty retreat. "Anyone who has a lick of sense will tell you to stay far away from that place. Why would you want to go there?"

"It's a matter of life and death," I said tightly. "Now will you please find us someone else to ask?"

Aelor gave me a dubious look, then introduced us to another captain. We talked to ten more, all friendly, capable-looking men who at first seemed extremely interested, but abruptly said no the moment they learned where we were going. I even increased the price several times, and still couldn't get anyone to bite.

"There's got to be more than ten captains," I said, desperation coloring my voice as the last man rejoined his friends, his back turned pointedly in our direction. "Who else can we talk to? Money is truly no object. We'll pay whatever we need, but we have to get to that island."

Aelor sighed. "All the captains I've introduced you to are honest, sensible men with good reputations. There are less...honorable men who will do anything for a price, but perhaps you should heed these men who've all told you the same thing."

"I wish we could," Halldor said, "but we have to get to that island." He palmed a few more coins and discreetly showed them to the man. "These are yours, but only if you can help us secure a ship."

Aelor looked torn, and part of me sympathized with him.

He was a good man, and his honor told him he should refuse, that he wanted no part in helping us with what he saw was a doomed endeavor. But this was also more money than he made in several months, and with two children to feed, he couldn't afford to turn it down.

"This way," he finally said.

The man led us to another tavern a few blocks away from the port. This place was much smaller than the last, with dirty, sticky floors, beat-up furniture that had seen quite a few bar fights, and beneath the smell of booze and unwashed bodies were traces of piss and vomit.

Halldor tensed as eyes turned toward us. The men here were less friendly, their eyes sharp and assessing as we walked to the bar, and more than a few eyed the pouch tied to my belt.

But I'd been in places like this plenty of times, and I knew how to behave. Casually, I let my hand drift to the dagger strapped to my thigh, letting them know that I wasn't an easy mark. Then I slid onto a ratty bar stool, leaned over the counter, and ordered a drink.

When the barkeep—a rough man with a shaved head whose arms and neck were covered in tattoos—brought me my tankard, I slugged the drink back in one go, ignoring the fact that it stripped off a layer of skin as it slid down my throat. Slowly, I lowered the tankard to the counter as I met the man's eyes, giving myself time to recover my voice. Then I leaned in and asked, very politely, which man in here owned the largest ship.

As Aelor translated my question, the barkeep's eyes flickered to the room behind me. "That one," he said in heavily accented Elantian, and I turned in the direction he nodded.

A man with long, dirty blond hair wearing a tri-corner hat and a long, oiled coat sipped slowly from his tankard as he watched us from the far corner of the room. He wore several hoops in each ear, and a tattoo of a sea serpent crept up the side of his neck. He was handsome in a rakish sort of way, and his cruel lips curved into a half smile as he studied me with seafoam green eyes that were too sharp for my liking.

"Absolutely not." Aelor grabbed my arm. "That's Captain Drakis!"

"And what's wrong with Captain Drakis?" I asked mildly, not taking my eyes away from the man.

"Officially he's a privateer, but everybody knows he and his crew illegally seize ships and cargo all the time." Aelor's fingers dug into my upper arm hard enough to bruise. "Please, Miss, let me find you someone else, anyone else."

I arched my eyebrow at him. "Can you find anyone else?" I asked, turning back to him.

"I—"

"Excuse me," Drakis said pleasantly. Somehow, he'd already managed to cross the room and stood solicitously at my side. "Is this man bothering you?" His seafoam eyes dropped to the hand clenched around my arm.

Aelor immediately dropped my arm as if he'd been burned. "We were just leaving," he said stiffly, making to move off the bar stool.

"Actually, my friend was just telling me that you're a captain who owns a very large ship." I gave Drakis a flirtatious smile, allowing my eyes to travel up and down his lean frame in a slow, deliberate once-over. "Do you think you could tell me exactly how large, Captain?"

"Large enough for your needs, I should think," Drakis said with a smirk as both Halldor and Aelor sputtered behind me. He eased his hip onto the stool next to me, his eyes never leaving mine. "What is it you're looking for, exactly?"

"My friend and I are looking for someone to take us someplace very special," I said sweetly. "Have you heard of a place called the Hellmouth?"

Those green eyes flickered, the only sign that Drakis was shocked. "Not exactly the best place for a holiday," he drawled, his gaze briefly switching to Halldor's. The two men seemed to size each other up for a minute before he turned back to me. "Why me, sweetheart? The *Borcas* is large, but you need speed more than size if you want to reach the Hellmouth before the winds change."

"We've got some large cargo," I said with a shrug, not missing the glint that entered Drakis's eyes. "I had the impression you aren't a man who asks a lot of questions," I added pointedly.

"You'd be right about that." Drakis gave me a cheerful grin. "The only question I need to know the answer to is if you're stingy. I charge twenty pieces of gold to get you there, and twenty-five to get you back. Unless you're not coming back?"

"Oh, we'll need a return journey for sure." I kept my tone light, not wanting to betray the very real fear that we might not come back from this at all.

"Forty-five pieces is robbery," Aelor growled. "But then again, you specialize in that, don't you, Drakis?"

Drakis narrowed his gaze on Aelor. "The voyage to the Hellmouth is fraught with dangers. The unpredictable winds and stormy weather, not to mention the sea monsters, are likely the reason everyone else has turned you down, haven't they?" He gave me a sly grin. "Otherwise, this stickler would have never brought you to me."

"Forty-five pieces sounds more than fair," I said before Aelor could piss off the privateer and ruin the only chance we had. "But we need to leave tomorrow morning. Oh, and just so you know," I added with a smile, "we'll be bringing four more companions aboard. I hope that's all right with you?"

Drakis shrugged. "Makes no difference to me as long as you pay." He held his hand out. "I'll need ten coins now, so my men and I can gather supplies and prep for the voyage. My ship is the one with the sea serpents," he added. "You can't miss it."

"Done." I dropped the coins into his outstretched hand. "Pleasure doing business with you, Captain."

There was a long silence as Drakis walked out of the tavern, whistling cheerfully.

"You are out of your mind," Aelor grumbled from behind me. "You do realize you've just signed your death warrant, don't you?"

I turned around and dropped the remaining coinage Halldor had promised Aelor into his front pocket. "Thank you for your help today, sir," I said, ignoring the thunderous look on his face. "I'm sure you'll be wanting to get home to your family now."

The former sailor stomped out of the tavern in a huff, muttering something in another language that I had a feeling was very uncomplimentary.

"You know," Halldor said as we left the tavern, "the man does have a point. That Drakis guy might have a pretty face, but he's no good. I wouldn't be surprised if we showed up at his ship tomorrow and he told us that he had no recollection of ever meeting us."

"I doubt that'll happen," I said as we turned a corner, heading back to the inn. "I saw the look in his eyes when we mentioned we had a large cargo. He's going to want to get it—and us—aboard his ship before he tries to rob us."

Halldor was silent for a split second before he let out a raucous laugh. "So that's the game you're playing, eh?" he chortled. "Well, they're going to get a very big surprise indeed when they find out exactly what their large cargo is."

In much better spirits, the two of us returned to the inn to tell Rhia and Tibo what had happened. The two of them were in the small dining room downstairs, eating a hearty breakfast, and seemed extremely annoyed when we sat next to them.

"You should have woken me up," Rhia accused as I snatched up her glass of juice and took a long draught. "We didn't have any way to contact you!"

"We did leave a note," I said mildly as I put the empty glass of juice down. A serving girl came by and Halldor and I ordered eggs and toast.

"Besides," Halldor said with a smile, "I think your body is really appreciating that sleep. Not that you weren't determined before, but now you look like you're ready to take on the world."

Rhia snorted. "That's the nicest way I've ever heard a man describe an angry woman." She lifted her refilled glass to her lips. I had the distinct feeling she was trying to hide a smile.

"So, you're leaving tomorrow?" Tibo said apprehensively. He chased the remaining bits of food on his plate with a fork, and I could tell from the hunched set of his shoulders that he was afraid we were going to abandon him. "Am I coming with you?"

"No," I said gently. "But I think I've finally found a place for you to go."

We finished breakfast, and the four of us went down to the docks.

"I don't want anything more to do with you," Aelor barked as we walked into his shop. He was sitting on the stool behind the counter, his rough hands flying as he busily mended a net. But his eyes widened as he caught sight of Rhia and Tibo. "Skies," he swore as he jumped to his feet. "You're taking a child to the Hellmouth?"

"Not if I can help it," I retorted. "Believe it or not, I'm not an idiot. The three of us can deal with whatever Drakis decides to pull. But Tibo..." I trailed off as I looked down at the little boy, who was staring apprehensively at Aelor. "We rescued him from pirate slavers a week ago, and we've been trying to find someone to take him in. As much as I know he'd like to come," I added, ruffling his hair fondly, "the Hellmouth is no place for a twelve-year-old."

"You want me to take him?" Aelor asked. He was silent for a moment, and then, slowly, he walked around the counter and crouched to meet Tibo at eye level. "What's your full name, boy?"

"Tibo Buoni," he said, bravely meeting Aelor's gaze. The boy gave the older man a frank assessment, taking in his well-made but old shirt and trousers, his close-shaven salt-and-pepper hair, and his skin weathered by salt and sea. "Are you a sailor?" he asked.

"Once," Aelor said. "Now I run my shop here, so I can be close to my wife and children." He sat back on his heels, his gaze thoughtful. "My kids are still too young to be away from their mother, but you look old enough to help me out in the shop. Is that something you would be interested in?"

Tibo hesitated. "Would you pay me?"

"I'd give you a roof over your head, clean clothes, and food in your belly. And my wife will smother you with hugs and kisses until you can't stand them, and stuff you so full of food at night I'll have to roll you out of bed every morning."

Tibo giggled. "That sounds nice," he said, but he turned to me, a question in his eyes.

I nodded. "Aelor's a good man." To Aelor, I added, "Tibo hopes to become a ship's captain someday."

"Ah." Aelor's eyes lit with understanding as he rose. "Well, I can care for the boy until he's old enough to begin an apprenticeship. There are many fine captains here in Roccar. We'll find you a good crew to sail with if that's what you're after, boy. Does he have any belongings?" he asked me.

"Just the clothes on his back," I said, but I handed him a purse. "And this."

Aelor's eyes widened as he opened the drawstring pouch, and he let out a low whistle. "That's enough to feed and clothe him until he's an adult."

"And some for you and your family, too, as thanks for taking him in." I lowered my voice. "I'm trusting you to spend it wisely."

Aelor gave me a long look. "I don't know what your business

is on that island," he finally said, "but it's clear you're not as stupid as I thought you were." He tucked the money behind the counter. "I'll take good care of him."

"Are...are you leaving me now?" Tibo asked in a small voice. He looked up at me, tears glimmering in his eyes.

"Yes." I dropped to my knees, blinking back tears of my own as he rushed into my open arms. "I wish I could say that we'll meet again, but we probably won't."

"I know," he said quietly, pitching his voice low so the others couldn't hear. "I just wish I could have said goodbye to the dragons."

"Tell Tibo I'm sorry I couldn't hug him, but I'm glad he's going to a good family," Lessie said. I could feel her sadness in the bond. As the one who'd rescued Tibo, she would miss him the most.

I relayed the message, and Tibo smiled. "I'm glad I got the chance to see dragons at least once in my life," he said, pulling away. "You're going to be careful, right?"

"We'll do our best." I smiled, trying to ease the worried look in Tibo's eyes. "Lessie and the others will keep us safe. But you have to promise not to mention anything about them to the others until we're gone, okay?"

He nodded. "I understand."

I gave him a moment to say goodbye to Halldor and Rhia, and then the three of us headed out to prepare for the voyage.

"I hope that man keeps his word," Halldor said. "There's no doubt he's a good man, but even good men can be swayed by greed, and we did give him a lot of gold."

"I think he'll be all right," Rhia said confidently. She stopped by a stall selling exotic colorful fruits, and plucked up a large, round fruit with yellow and green stripes to examine. "Aelor didn't lie about anything he said, so I know his intentions are true."

"Either way, it's better than taking a child to the Hellmouth," I said. And, if nothing else, at least the boy would be able to sleep soundly again, away from Zakyiar's influence.

As we walked, the piece of heart seemed to drag me down, slowing my stride. I wondered if the dragon god could only reach us in our dreams, or if there were other ways he would try to thwart us.

No point in worrying about it now, I told myself. We would find out soon enough once we were underway.

EIGHTEEN

Halldor, Rhia, and I spent the rest of the afternoon buying supplies and going over our plan with the dragons until we ironed out the details. Despite my worries, we enjoyed walking around the port city, sampling the exotic wares, and even buying a few carvings and vividly colored scarves as souvenirs.

"It's kind of funny, isn't it," Rhia giggled as we examined a trio of dragon carvings. They were each two feet tall, and the dragons had four sets of small wings spaced across their long, serpentine bodies. "These people don't really know what real dragons look like, do they?"

"I think they model them off the sea serpents that pirate captain was talking about," Halldor said. He traced the carving's long, undulating body, which was really shaped more like a snake than a dragon. "I really hope we don't encounter one of these on the open sea. I've heard the bigger ones can wrap their entire body around a ship and crush it."

The mental image that conjured sent a shudder through me. "It's a good thing we'll have three real dragons to fight them off, isn't it?"

"True." Halldor smirked. "Kiethara would love to tussle with a sea serpent. She's always spoiling for a fight."

Great. Another hothead to deal with. But then again, Halldor was a bit of a hothead himself, so I wasn't really surprised to learn that his dragon was, too. "As long as she doesn't go out of her way to provoke a fight, that's okay with me," I said dryly.

Naturally, I dreamed of sea serpents and thunderstorms that night. But though I could feel the dragon god's malevolence brushing against my mind, twisting my dreams into nightmares, neither he nor Salcombe made an appearance, and I slept through without waking. I wondered if that meant he was occupied elsewhere, or if he simply didn't feel up to torturing me that night.

Maybe he's just run out of creativity, I joked to myself, and then squashed that thought. If the dragon god was listening to my thoughts, the last thing I needed to do was challenge him to make my nightmares even more horrific than they already were.

The three of us bathed and dressed at first light, and met Captain Drakis at six in the morning, as agreed. It wasn't hard to find his ship. It was easily one of the biggest in the bay, constructed of some kind of black wood, and as promised, the mast sported large red sails with twisting sea serpents on them.

"Morning," Drakis called, lifting his cap in greeting as he watched us from the deck rail. His sharp gaze swept over us as we boarded the ship, and I knew he was wondering why we had packed so lightly. "Someone bringing your luggage along?" he asked casually.

"It's with the rest of our party," Halldor said. "They'll be joining us once we're underway."

Drakis scowled. "You expect us to load up your cargo once we're at sea, from another ship?" he demanded. "That's not going to be easy."

"You let us worry about that," I said sweetly as I handed him the remaining portion of his payment. "All you need to worry about is making sure this ship gets to the Hellmouth."

"If you say so." Drakis shrugged as he pocketed the money, then whistled. "This is Cronis, my first mate. He'll show you to your cabins while we get underway."

Drakis's first mate was a hulking monster of a man, with a smashed face, several missing teeth, and a thick accent we could barely understand. Halldor immediately put his body in front of Rhia as he approached us, but the man barely gave her a glance as he led us to the small cabins belowdecks that we'd been given.

"These are surprisingly clean," Rhia said as we inspected the spaces. They were small, with room for a narrow twin bed, chest of drawers, and a washstand, but more than sufficient for our needs. "I thought pirates were dirty people."

"Don't let them hear you say that," Halldor said under his breath. "Privateers can get real touchy about that kind of thing, even if they really are pirates."

"Sorry." Rhia's cheeks colored. "Do you think it's safe for us to leave our stuff here?"

"We don't have much," I said, eyeing the water and food supplies we'd brought. But the last thing I needed was for the pirates to tamper with our stuff, so I used my lockpick to seal the doors, then went above deck to watch as we set sail.

It took a few more minutes, but we finally took off, our sails catching a favorable wind. I sighed in relief as we sailed out of the harbor and smiled as we passed a rocky outcropping where a large group of sea lions sunned themselves. So far, Drakis hadn't given us much trouble. I had no doubt he'd get nasty on us at some point, maybe demand more money, but he'd quickly change his tune once Lessie and the others arrived.

"Zara!" Rhia cried. "Look!"

I turned back to the sea lions just in time to see an enormous sea serpent burst from the water. The sea lions barked frantically as they scrambled away, but the serpent struck fast, snatching one of the larger females up in its maw. The poor animal thrashed frantically, scoring the serpent with its huge tusks, but it was no match for the sea serpent. The larger beast's fangs pierced tough hide and blubber, raining blood onto the small patch of land, then abruptly disappeared beneath the waves, leaving nothing but a swirling red froth to indicate it had ever been there.

"Well." I cleared my throat, trying to banish that horrific sight from my mind as I turned back to Rhia. "At least we're not sea lions, right?"

"Right," Rhia echoed, her face white as a sheet.

"We'll be fine," Halldor said, putting an arm around Rhia's shoulder and turning her away from the scene of the attack. "Let's just try to enjoy the journey, okay?"

"Okay." She leaned into him with a long sigh.

A few of the sailors cast smug glances toward Rhia and

Halldor as they stood by the rail, and my stomach clenched as more than a few lingered on Rhia. But there was no need for me to butt in. Halldor's frigid glare was more than enough to keep the men moving. Halldor was tall, well-muscled, and a trained warrior, and few men aside from the first mate could easily take him. As he tightened his arm protectively around Rhia, I felt a twinge of jealousy. I certainly didn't need a man to protect me—for that matter, neither did Rhia—but Halldor's affections reminded me that Tavarian was absent.

What was he doing now, I wondered as I fingered the sapphire engagement ring. Had he finished his negotiations with Warosia? I hoped they'd managed to come to an agreement, but I knew these things were never simple. It had taken Tavarian over a month to get the Traggaran king to even give him an audience, and that might not even have happened if I hadn't orchestrated a series of events to turn King Zoltar against the Zallabarians.

Then again, the Warosians weren't our enemy. They wanted to ally with us against Zallabar, which already put us way ahead of the game.

"Miss." Captain Drakis's smug voice caught my attention, and I turned away from the railing to see him and ten of his men standing in front of us in a semi-circle. My blood iced over. All of them had drawn their cutlasses and pointed them straight at us. "I think we need to have a conversation."

I sucked in a deep breath, my hand drifting toward the dragon blade strapped to my leg. "Conversations typically don't involve swords."

He moved faster than I expected, the flat of his blade lifting my chin before I could raise my weapon against him. "Actually, in my experience, some of the best ones do," he drawled, a lazy gleam in his eye.

"You bastard," Halldor snarled, jabbing his own sword in Drakis's direction. "I knew you were going to try to cheat us."

"And yet you still boarded my ship anyway." The captain laughed. "You three really are idiots, aren't you?"

"Let me guess," I said, keeping my tone bored so he wouldn't sense my fear. Sweat trickled down my spine despite the chilly ocean breeze, and it took everything I had not to move when all I wanted was to disarm Drakis and run him through with my own weapon. "Now that you have us at your mercy, you're going to confiscate our supplies and sell us into slavery."

"Why, I couldn't have said it better myself." Drakis grinned at me, and the flash of too-white teeth sent a chill down my spine. "Although I might keep you," he said, slowly scraping his blade down the front of my shirt. He applied just enough pressure to make my blood run cold without actually pricking my skin. "I do have a soft spot for redheads, and it's been a while since I last kept a pleasure slave."

I was just about to tell him what he could do with that idea when a large shadow fell over the ship. "Dragons!" someone cried.

"Don't be ridic—" Drakis started when something large and very heavy landed on the poop deck. The pirates cried out as the ship began to capsize in that direction, cannons and equipment sliding toward the front. The blood drained from Drakis's face as he whipped his head in that direction, and I laughed as

Lessie grinned at him, displaying her terrifying maw of teeth to best advantage.

"Something wrong?" I asked pleasantly as Kiethara landed on the other end of the ship. The sailors screamed again as the boat began to list the other direction, and I used the distraction to knock the cutlass out of Drakis's hand. "I forgot to mention," I purred as I flicked my dragon blade out so that the edge rested against the side of his throat. "My three passengers are very large."

A third shadow passed over the ship, and the sailors scattered as Ykos landed in the middle, somewhat stabilizing things.

"I wouldn't do that," Halldor called as three of the men grabbed one of the cannons and pointed it at Ykos. "You might injure him, but the other two will set this entire ship on fire, and then where would you be?"

"You bitch!" Drakis's seafoam eyes blazed with fury as he bared his teeth at me. "You three are dragon riders, aren't you?"

"We sure are," I said cheerfully. "Now what was it that you were saying about getting us to our destination?"

Drakis's jaw worked for several moments as he tried to figure a way out of this. "If we kill you," he said slowly, "then your dragons will die too."

"Who told you that story?" I scoffed even as every hair on the back of my neck stood straight up. If the crew members moved fast enough, they could kill the three of us, and I had no idea if the dragons would be able to take their ship out before they died as well. "I assure you that if you harm even one hair on my head, Lessie will be more than happy to make your death very slow and very painful. Dragons aren't dumb beasts, you know. They're just as intelligent as humans, and they can be very inventive when it comes to revenge."

Drakis swallowed hard as he glanced at the three dragons. The rest of the sailors still had their weapons out, many trained on us, but they were shaking, and several of them sported some fetching trouser stains. "You can't sail this ship without us," he finally said.

"Aha." I winked at Rhia and Halldor. "Looks like he's finally catching on."

"Maybe," Rhia said with a wicked grin that surprised the hell out of me. "After all, we don't need all the sailors, do we? Dragons need a lot of food, and they get hungry pretty quickly. How many of them do you think they could eat without compromising the ship?"

"All right, all right!" Drakis finally threw up his hands in the air in surrender. He barked something at the other pirates, and they slowly lowered their weapons. "We'll take you to the Hellmouth."

"Excellent." I sheathed my weapon, then gave the captain a broad smile. "Now what do you say we rustle up some lunch?"

"That was insane," Halldor muttered later on as we sat on the poop deck. Lessie was curled up behind us, lazily watching the helmsman as he steered the ship. The three dragons had stayed exactly where they were, spread out across the ship so no one could try any funny business. "Completely and utterly insane."

"Maybe, but we're going to have quite the story to tell," Rhia said with a grin. I was happy to see that most of her fear had vanished. The confrontation with the pirates had exhilarated her, and she was still riding on the high of our victory. "It's not every day one can say they commandeered a pirate ship and its crew, can they?"

"No," I said with a chuckle as I leaned against Lessie's hide. Her warmth was a boon out on the open ocean like this. Though we were in a southern climate, the winds still made it chilly. "And we couldn't have done it without our dragons."

Lessie curved her neck inward to nuzzle me, but her mood was uncharacteristically solemn. *"We'll need to stay on our guard,"* she said. *"These men might be temporarily cowed into submission, but they are used to being in charge. It won't be long before they try to revolt."*

"I know." The hateful look Drakis cast our way every time he passed us was proof enough of that.

NINETEEN

"*Z*ara!" Lessie's strident voice pierced the murky dream. "*They're trying to escape!*"

I bolted upright in bed, then raced out the door, thankful I'd chosen to sleep fully dressed. "Rhia! Halldor!" I yelled as I raced up the stairs, but they were already behind me, woken by their own dragons.

"Damn you!" Captain Drakis swore as Lessie stood in front of the lifeboats. Two of them were already in the water, I noted, rowing away, but thankfully Lessie had headed off the captain himself before he could get on board. "Move out of the way!" he snarled, brandishing his sword at Lessie.

"Do you have a death wish, Captain?" I asked, genuinely curious as I strolled up to him. The captain whirled around to face me, sword pointed in my direction, but Lessie roared so loudly that he dropped the weapon immediately, his face turning sheet white in the moonlight.

"You can't keep us here," he snapped, straightening his spine.

I had to give the man credit—he had to be scared out of his mind, but he met my gaze squarely and didn't tremble. "There's not enough food or water on board for all of us and three dragons."

"That's why we brought extra supplies," I said pleasantly. "Besides, we're going to pass Laoras on our way to the for—" I nearly said "forge," then cleared my throat. "The Hellmouth, and we'll be able to stock up on extra water and food there."

The captain crossed his arms, his green eyes glittering as he studied me. "What was that you were about to call it?" he asked. "The force? The form?"

I gritted my teeth. "None of your business."

"Oh, I think it is my business." He took a step toward me, ignoring Lessie's warning snarl. "Your dragon isn't going to kill me for asking questions, not when you need me to run this ship," he snapped. "What is it you're looking for on that island? Treasure?"

I glared at him. "I thought I made it clear to you when I hired you that I wanted someone who wouldn't ask questions. Now either you tell your men to get their asses back to the boat, or our dragons will bring them back. And if they have to do that, I can't promise that they won't eat a few of them as a midnight snack."

The captain turned on his heel, then rushed over to the railing and started shouting at the men. I let out a silent sigh of relief when the sailors reluctantly rowed back to the boat. While it was true we probably didn't need all of them, the last thing I needed was for someone important to leave the ship if something went wrong.

"The next time this happens," I said quietly to Drakis as the lifeboats were hoisted back onto the ship, "I'm going to tie you up and strap you to Kiethara's chest." I gestured to the large red dragon at the other end of the ship who watched us with glittering gold eyes. "A dragon's chest is the hottest part of its body, where the fire sits, ready to be unleashed at a moment's notice. Oh, it's not hot enough to roast your balls off," I said with a vicious smile as Drakis's face went white again. "But you'll be very uncomfortable, that I can guarantee."

"You're a stone-cold bitch," Drakis muttered. "In other circumstances, I think the two of us might have been good friends."

I snorted. "We're never going to be friends. But if you quit trying to undermine me, we might all be alive by the end of this."

The next morning, the sailors were even surlier than usual. True, they kept the ship on course, and they didn't try to fight us, but the slop they served us for breakfast was barely edible, and we had to shout at them several times for them to even acknowledge us when we tried to give an order.

"I guess we can't really blame them," Halldor said dryly. "And threatening to kill them for serving us gruel isn't going to change anything."

Despite their hatred of us, the sailors were reluctantly fascinated by the dragons. From our travels through the continent, it was obvious that no one had ever seen a dragon before, and the sailors were taken in by their iridescent scales and powerful wings. They loved to watch the dragons fly over the ocean, hunting serpents and other large sea animals for their dinner, and they often placed bets whenever the dragons got into a battle with a sea serpent.

"By the dragon," Rhia muttered as Ykos landed on the deck, half a serpent dangling from his maw. He dropped the long, bloody piece of flesh on the deck, and the sailors watched in horrified amazement as he tore into it with relish. "It took me a bit of time to get used to watching him eat fresh kills, but this is a whole new level of gross."

"Better him eating the serpent than the serpent eating us," Halldor said, and I shuddered as Lessie landed next to him with the other half, which included the intact head. Was it just me, or was that thing still wriggling? "I think that if I walked over to that thing right now, it would still try to eat me," he added.

We made it to Laoras, and Rhia and I went ashore with the captain and five other men to get supplies. Ykos and Kiethara stayed with Halldor aboard the ship to make sure the sailors stayed in line, while Lessie flew overhead to discourage Drakis and his sailors from trying anything with us. The locals were terrified of Lessie's presence, but that actually ended up working in our favor. The merchants were very quick to help and gave us what we needed without haggling, clearly wanting to get us out of there as soon as possible.

"You know, I thought your dragons were going to be a pain in the ass, but they're actually quite handy," Drakis said as we returned to the ship. "Usually our ship takes damage from the sea serpents whenever we go this far south, but so far, we've survived this trip intact. Maybe we'll make it to the Hellmouth in one piece after all."

When we set sail again, despite being held hostage on their

own ship, the crew was in good spirits. For once, the cook made a decent meal, and this time the dragons didn't even detect any poison in the portions served to us.

"I wonder what's going to be waiting for us," Halldor said as we stood at the railing, looking out at the ocean. We were still too far away to see the Hellmouth, but my skin tingled as I imagined it rising up from the sea, a black volcano rumbling its displeasure at the sight of humans drawing near. "Do you think Derynnis will even let us inside?"

"He'd better," Rhia grumbled. "We didn't come all this way just to be stonewalled at the entrance."

"We'll dig a hole in the side of the volcano if that's what we have to do to get in," I said, though I really hoped it didn't come to that. I had a feeling the death god would take even less kindly to us breaking into his home than he would to us knocking on the door.

The next five days of sailing were rough. During the days, we were assailed by terrifying storms full of lightning that seemed determined to steer us off course, and by night, we were pummeled with horrible nightmares from the dragon god. On the second night, we were awoken by sailors trying to break down the doors of our cabins, only to blink at us in bewilderment the moment we disarmed them, a bleary look in their eyes as if they'd only just awakened.

"*It's the dragon god,*" Lessie hissed, her wings furled as we battled through yet another storm. Lightning arced across the boiling sky, briefly illuminating her body before all but those fiery eyes melted back into the darkness. "*He's the cause of these storms, the reason these pirates tried to kill everyone in their sleep."*

"I know," I said wearily as crew members rushed across the deck, following the shouted orders from their captain. Drakis was standing on the upper deck, fighting against the storm with everything he had as he wrestled with the helm. His coat and hair whipped around his body, and I wondered if it was some kind of sorcery that kept his tri-cornered hat firmly on his head. *"But if the worst the dragon god can do is terrorize us in our sleep and throw a little weather our way, then he's not as strong as we feared. Besides, we're almost there."* Only one more day of sailing, and we'd finally reach land.

But Lessie gave me a wary look. *"I wouldn't be too sure of that,"* she said. *"A lot can happen in twenty-four hours."*

The storm finally broke with the dawn, and I went belowdecks with Rhia to get some sleep along with half the crew, while Halldor stayed up to make sure the other half didn't try anything at the last minute. But I'd only managed to doze for an hour when Lessie awakened me.

"Zara." Her voice was tight with nerves. *"We've got company."*

"Company?" I rubbed at my bleary eyes. *"Who the hell would be out here in the middle of nowhere with us?"*

"I'm not sure. But it's an Elantian warship, and its approaching very fast. Halldor says there are close to one hundred men aboard."

Shaking the cobwebs of sleep from my head, I dragged myself upstairs to see what was going on.

"It's unnatural," Drakis said, using a spyglass to study the warship from the starboard rail. "That ship is approaching far too quickly given how calm the winds are. Look at us. We're barely moving ten knots. That ship has to be going at least twenty."

Fear knotted my stomach, and I slid my goggles on to get a better look. Unfortunately, the ship was still too far away for me to see much, but the flags appeared to be Elantian. Still...

"*Lessie, let's go check this out with Ykos. Kiethara is going to stay by the ship, but she should fly up too, just in case.*"

"*Will do.*"

Rhia and I jumped onto our dragons' backs and took off. The sailors cried out as we lifted off, and I glanced back to see that the ship had risen ten feet. The dragons had been weighing it down more than I thought.

As we arrowed toward the Elantian ship, it suddenly put on a burst of speed.

"*Zara!*" Lessie cried, her voice full of alarm. "*It's Salcombe at the helm!*"

"*I know,*" I growled. The bastard stood behind another sailor, his arms raised. A black glow surrounded him, and I had a feeling he was using the dragon god's power to create the strong backwind that was giving the ship its frightening speed.

"Halldor," I said into the earpiece. "Tell Drakis to get those cannons ready!"

"He's already on it," Halldor said. "Do you need us to come out there with you?"

"No. Stay with the ship."

Cannon fire exploded from the warship at the same time Lessie and Ykos dove toward it. The warship was technically too far away to fire on the *Borcas*, but somehow the cannonball managed to cross the distance, at least judging by the sound of splintering wood and shrieks coming from behind us. Ignoring it, Lessie and Ykos opened their maws wide and unleashed a torrent of fire on the enemy ship.

A black shield flared to life around the warship, and the flames harmlessly scurried along it. Rhia and I exchanged horrified looks as the flames disappeared beneath the waves, leaving the ship completely unharmed.

"We're screwed," Halldor said into my ear over the sound of more cannon fire. Twisting around, my heart sank into my shoes at the sight of the *Borcas*. The poop deck had been badly damaged, and one of the masts was broken in half. "Completely, totally screwed."

"Like hell we are," I snarled, turning toward Rhia. She nodded when I explained what I wanted, and the two of us flanked the port side of Salcombe's ship. Our dragons began to beat their wings furiously. The men aboard Salcombe's ship shouted in dismay as their ship was pushed back, in the opposite direction of the *Borcas*.

"Tell Kiethara to do the same thing, but in the other direction," I told Halldor through the earpiece. "Let's get as much distance between us and Salcombe's ship as you can."

"Excuse me." Drakis was suddenly speaking in my ear, and I gathered he'd snatched Halldor's earpiece away from him. "Not that I'm complaining that you seem to be sacrificing yourself to save us, but how do you plan on reaching the Hellmouth if you stay behind while we get away?"

"I'm hoping we can figure out a way to defeat these bastards and then catch up with you," I said, glancing down at the ship. To my dismay, it looked like Salcombe was already fighting back—he circled his arms in a forward direction, using the dragon god's dark power to rally the winds behind their ship.

"That may be a bit difficult, considering he's got a magic shield and cannons that seem to defy gravity," he said dryly. "However, I might just have a plan."

Lessie snorted when Drakis told us what it was. *"That's never going to work,"* she protested. *"You can't just create something like that out of thin air."*

"What do you think?" I said to Rhia.

"It's insane." But she grinned at me, her chestnut hair whipping around her face like a dark banner. "Insane, but also brilliant. I've read something about this before, and I think—"

"We don't have time for a science lesson," Drakis interrupted. "Your dragons are starting to tire. It's now or never."

I sighed. He was right. I could feel Lessie flagging from the strain of beating her wings while staying in one place. *"You think we can do this?"* I asked Lessie.

"Yes. But we're going to need Kiethara."

Kiethara winged her way toward us, and the three dragons flew in a circle, with Lessie and me in the lead. With their wings spread as far as they could, the dragons chased each other round and round the ship, breathing streams of fire into the air to heat it up. Salcombe scowled up at us and shouted orders for the crew to fire on us, but the cannons flew harmlessly into the ocean, angled too far down to reach us.

"Do you really think you can find a way to penetrate my shield?" His voice echoed in my head, dripping with malevolence. "I have two of the relics now, and they augment my power even as the ones you have continue to drain you. You're never going to win."

"I may not have a powerful dragon god on my side," I said. We passed close enough to lock eyes, and I gave him a fierce grin. "But I've got something better—nature."

A large wave suddenly battered the ship, and Salcombe slammed into the railing, nearly going overboard.

"Faster," I urged Lessie as the water churned, following the same pattern as the dragons. The waves rose higher and higher, tangling with the heated air, and Salcombe's sailors swore as they realized what was happening.

"Widen the circle!" I shouted, and Lessie banked right as the swirling water continued to rise. Soon it was no longer a circle of crashing waves, but a twisting cylinder of wind and water that howled across the opening sea, taking on a life of its own.

"Yes!" Rhia cried, face flushed and eyes blazing as she punched the air. "We did it!"

"You're damn right we did," Halldor shouted as the cyclone turned toward us. "Now let's fly!"

The dragons put on a burst of speed, flying back toward the ship as fast as they could. My heart pounded as the cyclone roared behind us, and I swore under my breath, wondering if Salcombe had somehow managed to harness the winds to his advantage.

"It would be just like him to do something like that," Lessie snarled. Her body trembled beneath me. She couldn't take much more. *"Isn't there anything we can do?"*

"Maybe if Tavarian were here," I said. He might have been

able to use his magic to change the cyclone's direction, but he was a world away. *"Either way, we've got to get back to the ship before you collapse. If we die, well, the gods will just have to find a different champion."*

We turned toward the ship, and the three of us landed heavily, nearly launching several pirates overboard.

"I didn't mean for you to bring the storm to us!" Drakis yelled over the shrieking winds. The ship was in chaos as the sailors fought to secure everything on deck from the rapidly increasing winds.

"Don't look at me like that!" I yelled back. I dodged out of the way as a loose cannon barreled toward me, then swore. "This cyclone thing was your idea!"

We were still bickering when lightning sizzled through the air, followed by a deafening thunderclap. I braced myself, almost sure that this was the end, but the winds shifted, and the cyclone inexplicably began spinning in the other direction, headed north, Salcombe's ship still trapped within.

"Wha—" Halldor sputtered as the winds around us quieted. "What just happened?"

Rhia laughed at the thunderstruck look on his face. "I think that might have been a little divine intervention," she said, her eyes twinkling as she looked at me.

As soon as she had said the words, Caor's smug voice echoed in my head. *"If you think we're going to let you out of your champion duties so soon, you can think again, little mortal."*

I snorted. *"Just because you're thousands of years old doesn't mean you get to call me 'little.' You're not that much bigger than me."*

"If that's your way of saying thank you, then I think you need to work on your gratitude. Perhaps praying to me several times a day, with offerings, would be a good start. Building a few statues in my honor would be nice, too."

I was saved from having to come up with a retort for that absurd idea by Drakis. "I'm still not sure about all this divine intervention crap," he said, folding his arms across his chest. He was quite disheveled, his face smeared with soot, his hair tangled, and he finally seemed to have lost his hat. "What happened there was a miracle, I'll give you that, but two of our masts are down and I've lost five men. How are we going to make it to the Hellmouth now?"

"We don't have to," Rhia said as the last of the storm disappeared. The clouds parted, and several crew members gasped as the volcanic island loomed in front of us, barely half a day's journey away. "Looks like the gods gave us a push. We're here."

TWENTY

Even with only one mast left, the *Borcas* still managed to limp into a deep bay on the island that served as a natural harbor. Steep hills of volcanic stone rose all around us as we beached the ship, and a greenish haze tinted the sky, blocking out much of the natural sunlight.

"This place is foul," Lessie growled as we stared up at the volcano. Despite the haze, it was perfectly visible, a behemoth of a mountain that loomed over us, casting long shadows across the rest of the island. The green haze seemed to come from the smoke drifting out of the top of the volcano. *"The air here is poisoned by whatever is coming out of that accursed mountain."*

"Yeah, it doesn't look good." I didn't seem to be affected, but Rhia and Halldor looked a bit green around the gills, and I could feel the nausea roiling in Lessie's stomach. I could only imagine that the air quality would get even worse the closer we got. Would we even be able to breathe? What would that smoke do to us?

"Well, you've made a good run of it," Drakis said, slinging an arm around my shoulder. He gave me a grin, but he was looking a bit ill himself. "And I will have the distinction of saying I'm the only captain who's ever made it to the Hellmouth, if we ever get back to civilization. But unless you want to risk your entire team being poisoned, I don't see how you can go any farther."

I batted his hand away as his sneaky fingers went for the pouch tied to my waist, and he laughed. "Just because you're trying to distract me from my impending doom doesn't mean you can steal from me," I said mildly. "I was a thief in my former life, and I know all the tricks."

"You won't have to worry about the smoke," Caor said, stepping out from behind a rocky outcropping. Drakis and his men immediately drew their swords, but Caor continued to stroll toward us as if the men were waving feathers instead of blades. "Your amulet will protect you from the worst of it. Your friends, however, will not survive it. You're going to have to go it alone."

"Alone?" Halldor yelled, incensed. "We've come all this way only to be told we have to sit on our thumbs and wait?"

"I'm not letting you go in there without me," Lessie snarled, snapping her teeth at Caor. *"I don't care what this slimy bastard says. You're not facing a death god by yourself."*

"Who is this guy, and where did he come from?" Drakis demanded. "Does he live on this island? Is he the reason you came?"

"In a manner of speaking," I said wryly. "Drakis, this is Caor. He's a messenger of the old gods and likes to think he can tell me what to do. He's also occasionally helpful."

"Occasionally?" Caor was highly offended. "I've saved your

life twice now, Zara. If not for me, Salcombe would have steered that cyclone directly into the *Borcas* and destroyed all of you. Not to mention, I gave you all a little boost to the island."

"Wait a minute," Drakis said faintly. "You're actually serious about all this."

"Unfortunately. He really is a god." I flipped a dagger into my hand and tossed it at Caor before anyone could blink. The blade sailed right through him and bounced off the stone behind him, then passed through him again before landing on the ground at his feet.

Scowling, Caor picked up the dagger. "Since I know you weren't deliberately trying to hurt me, I won't take that as an insult," he said as he handed it back to me.

"Guh..." Drakis sputtered, his eyes wide. "How can you touch things if daggers can pass through you?"

Caor winked. "One of the perks of being in two realms at once. Now listen closely," he said, a deadly serious expression on his face as he turned his attention to me, "because there are many dangers ahead, and I am only going to say this once."

"Are you sure you're ready for this, Zara?"

Rhia and I stood at the edge of a skeletal forest, about a mile away from the bay we'd camped in last night. After Caor had left, I'd taken a few hours to pack as many provisions and supplies as I could comfortably carry, then wrote letters to my friends and loved ones using parchment and ink from the

Borcas. There was nothing more that I could do—the only way now was forward.

"Ready as I'll ever be." I sucked in a deep breath as I glanced skyward, to the looming mountain waiting for me.

Lessie and I had taken a short flight last night to see what we could glean, and we'd managed to catch a glimpse of a glowing cavern about halfway up the side of the volcano before she'd been forced to retreat, hacking as her lungs rebelled against the toxic smoke.

"I actually got a surprisingly good night of sleep last night," I said. "I thought for sure that the dragon god would do his best to terrorize me again."

"I think Caor must have done something, because I didn't have any nightmares either," Halldor said. "Do you really think he's just a messenger god? He seems to have an awful lot of power."

I frowned. The thought that Caor might be lying about his identity had never occurred to me, but... "It could be he's been calling on the other gods to help us," I said. "After all, he is the messenger."

"And of course, the other gods wouldn't deign to speak to us directly." Lessie snorted as she nudged me in the back with her snout, and I turned around to hug her. She was still a bit weakened from last night's flight, but she'd insisted on coming this far with me. *"I'd like to send them a message to tell them what I think about forcing you into danger like this, without anyone to help."*

I laughed, scratching her under the chin. *"I'm pretty sure this is a rite of passage for all heroes and champions, at least according to every legend and myth I've ever read,"* I said as she purred beneath my ministrations. *"The hero might have help from friends for part of the journey, but the final battle is something they must face alone."*

"But you won't be alone," Lessie said. "No matter how far away you are, I will always be with you."

Tears stung the corners of my eyes as I hugged her tighter, then stepped away. *"I love you."*

"I know. Now go show that death god what for."

Rhia and I said our goodbyes. I adjusted the straps of my pack around my shoulders, then took my first step into the skeletal forest. The moment I did, the green haze seemed to close around me, cutting me off from my friends. My heart pounded loudly in my ears, the only sound I could hear anymore. The ebony branches reached toward me like ghostly hands, scraping against my skin and clothes. The sound the branches made as they snapped back into place echoed far too loudly in the dense quiet.

Relax, Zara, I told myself, taking deep, slow breaths as I forced myself to put one foot in front of the other. *They're just trees. They can't hurt you.*

Following Caor's instructions, I kept to the path, a thin strip of earth that glittered white, like crushed diamonds. It wound through the trees in a twisting path, and I was forced to take things slow since I could only see about ten feet in front of me. Murky voices whispered through the trees, unintelligible sounds belonging to disembodied voices. I couldn't understand what they were saying, but there was something hauntingly familiar about the cadence, and more than once my feet tried to stray from the diamond path of their own accord.

"Zara." A shadowy form flickered to my left, and I whipped around just as it vanished. "Zara, help me..."

"Rhia?" I called back, my palms growing sweaty as I tightened my grip around the handle of my dragon blade. Oh gods, had my friends decided to follow me into the forest after all? "Rhia, you have to turn back!"

"I... can't..." Rhia choked out, her words dissolving into hacking coughs. I caught another flicker of shadow, this time to my left. "Please, Zara, help..."

"Don't listen." Lessie's voice was a soothing balm in my head, calming my frayed nerves. *"Rhia is right here with me. What you're seeing and hearing are shadows and echoes, tricks of light and sound to make you stray from the path."*

"Right." I took another steadying breath and straightened my shoulders. Of course Rhia wasn't really here. She wouldn't have been able to make it this far, not when the green miasma was ten times thicker than it had been at the bay. *"Thanks, Lessie."*

"See?" I could hear the smile in her voice. *"I told you you're not alone."*

Those words, more than anything, warmed my heart and gave me courage. I pushed on, moving faster now, my steps sure now that I knew what to expect. Every time I heard a voice, saw a shadow, Lessie was there to remind me that none of it was real, that all that mattered was to stick to the path until I reached the base of the mountain.

I was doing so well until I rounded the bend and found myself standing in a very different place.

"You say none of this is real?" a woman asked as she knelt on the ground next to the body of a dead man. A waterfall of red curls hid her face as she rocked back and forth on her knees, clutching the man's lifeless hand in hers. "How can you say that, when I gave my life for yours?"

"Wh-who are you?" I stammered, an awful feeling curling in the pit of my stomach. The green haze in the air gave way to a different atmosphere, and suddenly I was standing in a narrow alley, the diamond path transformed to cobblestones. The scent of rotting garbage and urine assailed my nostrils, and beneath that was the thick, pervasive scent of fresh blood.

The woman lifted her head, sad green eyes meeting mine. "You know who I am, Zara."

I stumbled backward, a scream trapped in my throat at the sight of her neck, which had been slashed open. Blood poured out of the wound, covering the front of the simple blue dress she wore, but the woman smiled, opening her arms to me. "Won't you give me a hug, daughter? I've waited so long for you."

"She's not real, Zara. She's not real!"

But the voice screaming in my head was faint, coming from another place, another lifetime. Too stricken by shock to move, I sank to my knees until we were eye level. "What happened to you?" I choked out, trying not to stare at her neck. But gods, that wound... "Who did this to you?"

"I can't answer that," she said in that achingly sad voice. Her arms were still outstretched, and I stared at the simple band of silver around her ring finger. "I didn't know the men who killed us, and I haven't seen them in the afterlife since. But it doesn't matter anymore." A smile bloomed on her face, so like mine and yet not, chasing away the grief and the darkness. "You're here with us now. And you can stay with us forever."

Forever. The child in me ached for the promise in that word, in those open arms, and I inched forward, slowly. "But what about Father?" I asked, my gaze unwillingly switching to the man lying on the ground. He would have been handsome in death if his face wasn't frozen in a picture of horror. Wide gray eyes stared unseeingly at the sky, and his mouth was still open in a silent scream. "How can we be a family without Father?"

My mother smiled. "That's just a shadow," she said, and he disappeared with a wave of her hand. "Your father is waiting for us, inside the mountain. Come to me, Zara, and we can go see him. Together."

"Not...real..."

I closed the distance between us, wrapping my arms around my mother's slim frame. Closing my eyes, I buried my face in her hair, inhaling her sweet, floral perfume. Blood soaked the front of my shirt as she hugged me back, and for a minute I pretended that this was normal, that she was still alive and that this was a happy reunion.

And then I yanked a dagger from my belt and stabbed her in the heart.

"I'm sorry," I said as I pulled away, tears running down my face. The arms clutching at me were bone, long stripped of flesh, and the face looking back at me was desiccated, paper-thin skin stretched across a bony skull with empty sockets for eyes. "I wish I could follow you, but Caor warned me that if I followed any of the dead, they would lead me down the wrong path, and I would never come out of the Underworld again."

That desiccated face stretched into a smile that was terrifying and gentle all at once. "I'm so glad," she whispered in a voice like death as her body started to crumble away. "So glad that you've passed this first test. Keep going, daughter. I will be waiting for you at the end."

I knelt on the ground until her body turned to ash, until the ash was swept away by the miasma, until the cobblestones had transformed into the diamond path once more. And then I got to my feet, wiped the tears from my cheeks, and continued into the darkness.

TWENTY-ONE

By the time I made it to the base of the mountain, night had fallen. Exhausted but triumphant, I sat down heavily on a large block of volcanic stone, then took a swig from my canteen. The water was laced with an herb that promoted alertness and gave me a little boost of energy, something I would need as I was about to embark on the ascent.

"Are you sure you don't want to sleep for a bit?" Lessie asked. Her voice was calm, but I could feel the buzz of anxiety through the bond. She'd been out of her mind with worry during that encounter with the spirit that might or might not have been my mother—I still hadn't reconciled it in my head—and I couldn't blame her. If not for her faint warnings, for the hum of instinct in my head, I might have fallen for the spell that had been so expertly woven around me.

"There's no point," I said as I bit into one of the biscuits I'd packed. The food was dry and flavorless, but I choked it down anyway. *"The moment I shut my eyes, the dragon god is just*

going to haunt me in my sleep. Better not to give him the satisfaction."

"True," Lessie said. She was silent for a minute, then added, *"The pirates have managed to fix one of the masts. I think the ship will be ready to go by the time you come back."*

I steeled myself for an argument. *"If something happens with the volcano before I come back, Rhia and Halldor need to get on board and leave without me."*

Silence. Then, *"They're not happy about that idea."*

"And I'm not happy about them dying because the pirates decided to leave them behind," I snapped back. I had no idea what was going to happen once I entered the forge, if the death god would vent his anger out on the island should I do something to displease him. *"Now tell them to promise, or I'm not going into the mountain."*

The silence that followed was longer this time, and my heart pounded as I wondered if I would actually have to follow through on the threat. I'd come too far to give up now...but I didn't know how I'd be able to live with myself if Rhia and Halldor died on this island with me. The two of them could be good together if they were just given a chance, and the rest of the colony on Polyba needed their skills and experience. I'd be damned if I'd take them down with me just because they had some misguided sense of loyalty.

"They promised," Lessie finally said, *"but they say it's unnecessary, because you're going to come back. They also said that if you're not going to sleep to stop sitting around and start climbing."*

I laughed, picturing the cross look on Rhia's face. *"Gee, thanks. Tell them I appreciate the encouragement."*

I finished my biscuit and sat on the stone for a few minutes longer, letting the food settle. I was sitting high enough on the side of the mountain to see above the trees, but the miasma here was thicker than ever, especially now that night had fallen. If not for the amulet blazing on my chest, I doubted I'd be able to see anything at all, but the white light cut a path through the darkness, illuminating the rough terrain around me.

"All right," I said to myself as I got to my feet. I turned to confront the obsidian volcano and grasped the first handhold. "Time to climb."

It took three hours to reach the glowing cavern Lessie and I had spotted from the air, and by the time I hauled myself onto the ledge my body was shaking with exhaustion.

"Damn rocks," I grumbled as I fumbled a tin of salve from my pack. The rocky face of the mountain was sharp and jagged, and I'd been cut numerous times when my hands closed around a handhold that was just a little too sharp to be usable. Using precious water, I cleaned a large gash on my left palm, then smeared salve on it as well as on a few of the smaller cuts.

I sighed heavily at my shredded trousers. There were cuts on my legs too, and a particularly nasty one on the side of my thigh from when I'd lost my footing and had slid a good twenty feet down the side of the mountain. The curses I'd spewed as I'd been forced to climb that section again had been foul enough that even Drakis would have blushed if he'd been within earshot.

After I finished patching myself as best I could, I forced myself to my feet to get a better look at my surroundings. The cave was much wider and deeper than it had appeared from the outside, and the floor sloped down, leading somewhere deep within the mountain. The space held no torches but was illuminated by a red glow from somewhere beyond the slope. The light caught the glittering diamonds in the center of the floor that twisted and swirled, forming a large, circular symbol of an anvil and a scythe.

The reaper and the smith. Caor had told me this symbol would be waiting. This was definitely the right place.

Heat waves shimmered around me as I moved farther into the cave. I drew in shallow breaths, afraid the air would scorch my lungs. I knew it would be hot in here—this place was, after all, an active volcano—but this heat was beyond anything I'd ever experienced. Caor had assured me that as long as I wore the amulet, I would be able to survive it. My skin wasn't blackening to a crisp, but it still felt like I was roasting.

I walked on for twenty minutes, the air growing gradually hotter until I finally reached a chasm. I swallowed hard and peered over the edge, staring into the vast sea of lava waiting beneath me.

"Derynnis?" I shouted, my voice echoing in the vast space. "Please, I need to speak with you!"

When there was no answer, I called out for Lessie instead, who had been conspicuously silent since I'd entered the cave. She couldn't help me, but I felt shaky and needed some comfort, a mental hug so I could gather my wits and figure out what to do next.

But Lessie didn't answer, and when I reached through the bond, nothing was there.

"*Lessie?*" I called again, frantic now as the nightmare resurfaced. Had the dragon god gotten to her somehow, turning her against me and cutting off our bond? But no, how could he? He wasn't strong enough yet. I still had the pieces of the dragon heart... didn't I?

"Your dragon can't reach you here," a man said, scaring the daylights out of me as he appeared out of nowhere. I gaped at the shadowy figure as he hovered over the chasm, cloaked in a black robe and a hood that hid his face. "You've crossed into the realm of the dead now."

"Wonderful." I laid on the sarcasm thick, partially to hide my shaking insides. "Can you take me to Derynnis? I need to speak with him."

The figure was silent for a long moment. "This realm is not meant for the living," he said. "If you continue to remain here, you may not be able to leave again."

"If that's the price, then so be it." Opening one of the pouches, I grabbed the piece of heart I'd recovered in Barkheim and thrust it in the figure's direction. "I came here because I was told that this could only be destroyed in the Underworld."

I half-expected the figure to recoil, as Caor had once done when I'd tried to give him the piece of heart. But he merely floated there, unmoving, as he considered my words.

"That is a piece of the dragon god's heart," he finally said. "Where did you get such a foul thing?"

Tired, I sat cross-legged on the floor and told him the whole story. The figure listened silently, patiently, as I told him about the pieces of heart and that the other gods had named me their champion.

"Derynnis is expecting me. He showed me a... vision, or something, of my mother when I walked through the forest. He must know who I am and why I'm here."

"It is customary for a deity to search the soul of any person intruding on their domain," the figure said. There was no inflection in his voice whatsoever, and I couldn't tell if he was annoyed or amused. Who was this guy, anyway? Was he the death god, or just a messenger?

"Yes, well, can you tell me if he's judged me or not already?" I asked, growing impatient. Just how long could the amulet protect me from this unbearable heat? "Or at least tell me what I need to do. What if I throw this into the chasm?" I peered over the edge at the bubbling lava. "Is the heat from the lava enough to destroy it?"

"No," the figure said. "Only a god has the power to destroy such a powerful object." He paused. "Your cause is worthy enough, but you still need to prove that you are. You will need to prove yourself to Derynnis if you wish to gain his help."

"Of course I do." Was nothing ever easy? "I guess that first test in the woods doesn't count?"

"That was child's play," the figure said. "These next ones are the true challenges that will prove your mettle. If you can survive them, Derynnis will help you. But I would suggest you turn back while you still have your life. Humans are weak and fragile, and these tests were not designed for mere mortals."

"Yeah, well, I'm not a mere mortal," I said as I hauled myself to my feet. "I'm the champion of the gods, so that has to count for something. Now let's get on with it."

"Very well." The figure raised his arms, and a black, swirling mist surrounded me, blocking out all sight and sound. I barely had time to panic before the mist vanished, and I stood in the middle of a maze. At least I assumed it was a maze, judging by the high, narrow corridors with no ceiling that zigzagged in confusing directions. The walls were smooth and bare, with no footholds to climb up so I could get my bearings. Unlike in the skeletal forest, the floors were obsidian, with no crushed diamond path to lead the way.

"What the hell am I wearing?" I muttered as I walked, keeping one hand on the right wall. I wasn't sure that trick would work in this place, but it was the only one I knew, so I stuck with it. The death god had completely stripped me of my weapons and supplies, but he'd also stuck me in some old-fashioned gray tunic and sandals. The clothes were comfortable enough, but they were so light it almost felt like I wore nothing, and the sensation was a little disconcerting.

At least it wasn't sweltering in here, wherever this was. The air was neither hot nor cold—and was as smooth and silent as the stone walls rising up around me.

I walked for what felt like a mile before I came to a dead end. I would have turned back if not for the inscription carved into the wall.

"Of course it's not in any modern language," I grumbled as I squinted at the runes. The torches set into the walls provided some light, thankfully, but it was still fairly dark in the maze.

"Five men's strength...five men's length...yet a little boy can carry it easily. What am I?"

The runes glowed softly in response. I caught my breath, then let it out in a huff when nothing happened.

"I get it. A riddle." I tapped my foot as I thought about it. Something as long as five men and as strong...but a little boy could carry it...

"A rope," I said decisively. "It's a rope."

A rope unfurled from the top of the wall out of nowhere, and I grasped it with both hands. *Okay*, I thought as I hauled myself up and over the side. *Maybe this won't be so hard*. The rope didn't disappear when I reached the top of the wall, so I yanked it from whatever was anchoring it, looped it around my waist, hopped down, and continued on.

The rest of the riddles were similar, but yielded other rewards: a knife, a bow, a quiver of arrows, a sturdy shield, a longsword. On and on, until I was fully outfitted for battle. The only thing I was missing, I noted ruefully, was armor. I still wore the flimsy tunic and sandals, the straps of which chafed terribly against my skin.

I rounded a corner, then stopped in my tracks at the sight of another dead end. This wall was different from the others. Rather than a dull gray, this one was crafted of shimmering white stone, and had a door cut into it, though it had no handle.

"Forged and cut, yet blood is naught. Take me, set me, and you will be free. What am I?"

"A key," I said confidently, holding out my hand. One materialized instantly, along with a keyhole set in the door. Sucking in a breath, I palmed my newly acquired knife in one hand as I used the other to turn the lock.

I had no illusions about the maze. The riddles were too easy to pose a true challenge, which meant the real test lay beyond this one. These items were to prepare me for whatever I would face next.

But when the door swung open, no enemy waited beyond. Instead, I stepped into a large dining room with a twelve-foot rectangular table. The table stretched nearly the length of the room, and its wooden legs groaned under the weight of dozens of dishes. Roasted turkey, stuffed goose, glazed lamb, cakes and pies and more sides than I'd ever seen in my entire life, all piled on one table.

"Zara!" Jallis leaped up from the table, and I nearly toppled over in shock. My mouth fell open as I realized these were all dragon riders seated around the table. Rhia, Halldor, Kade, Ullion, Daria...on and on I counted the names, until I finally lost track. It seemed impossible that there were enough seats for this many people, yet somehow, they fit, eagerly digging into the feast laid out before me.

Jallis took me by the hand and dragged me to the table. "Come on, sit and eat!" he said jovially as he pulled out a chair for me. "You must be exhausted after walking around in that annoying maze for so long."

"I can't," I said, even as I took a seat. But my stomach growled, and I nearly whimpered when Jallis began piling my plate high with food. "Caor said that I couldn't eat or drink anything, or I'd be stuck in the dead realm forever."

"And what would be so bad about that?" A pair of strong,

warm hands settled on my shoulders, and my heart leapt into my throat as I twisted around to look into Tavarian's face. He smiled, his silver eyes full of tenderness. "All your friends are here, even Carina and the orphans." He nodded to the left side of the table, and I glanced over to see that, sure enough, they were here, attacking a bowl of chocolate pudding with relish. "It's warm and safe here, and there's plenty of food. What's the rush?"

"I have to finish the tasks Derynnis set out for me before Drakis finishes repairing the boat," I said. "If I don't, the pirates will leave without us, and Lessie and I will be stuck on that island with no way off."

Tavarian frowned. "What does that matter?" he asked as he sat next to me. He threaded his long fingers with mine, and temptation hit me like a firestorm. It would be so easy to let him tug me into his lap, to sink my hands into his silky black hair and kiss him until I couldn't remember my name.

But I did know my name, and I knew as sure as the sunrise that this wasn't real. Tavarian wasn't here with me, and even if he was, he would never discourage me from continuing on with my quest.

"Since we're all dead anyway," he was saying, "I don't really see the point—"

"Wait, what?" I pulled my hand from his and held it up. "What do you mean, since we're all dead anyway?"

He shrugged. "Well, all of us but you. You weren't on the island when the Zallabarians arrived. They brought a fleet of airships outfitted with more of those terrible shrapnel cannons, and a thousand men besides that. We didn't stand a chance."

Grief twisted his handsome features as he added, "I wonder if I will see Muza again. If I am dead, then he must be too. But do dragons get to go to the afterlife, when the gods have never cared for them? Or do they pass on into some other realm?"

"No." Tears scalded my eyes as I grabbed Tavarian's shoulders, my fingers digging in hard enough to bruise. "You're not Tavarian. You're lying."

"I wish I were." Those swirling silver eyes were heavy with sadness. "None of us made it out alive, Zara. The Zallabarians even killed the locals. Ironic, really, that death ended up uniting us when life could not. The chieftains finally banded together with us and we made our last stand at the base. But it wasn't enough, Zara. None of it is ever enough."

"Zara, are you okay?" Carina's hand landed on my shoulder, a sympathetic squeeze that wrenched a sob from me. Her eyes were wide with concern as I turned to look at her. "I thought you'd be happy to see us all here waiting for you, but you didn't even come and say hello?"

"I'm sorry," I croaked around a lump in my throat. I felt like I was being torn apart inside by an invisible shredder running repeatedly across my soul. Twisting around, I looked again at Rhia and Halldor, who were sitting at the foot of the table, laughing as they spoon-fed each other from a bowl of beef stew. How had they died? Had Drakis and his men turned on them, or had they braved the miasma to come looking for me because I'd been gone too long? "I've failed you all."

"You did your best, Zara," Jallis said, rubbing my back in soothing motions. The three of them crowded around me, and a weariness settled over me, rooting me to the chair. If they really were all dead, what was the point of continuing on? Let the gods find another champion to defeat Zakyiar. I was so tired of fighting, so tired of being hurt and scared. I just wanted to live in peace with my friends, with the man I loved.

And what about Lessie? a voice whispered in my head. *Is she not your best friend?*

The sound of Lessie's name was like a bucket of ice water being dumped on my head, and I jumped to my feet, heart pounding.

"No," I said in a trembling voice as I backed away. I couldn't feel Lessie through the bond, but I knew in my heart she was still alive. After all, I hadn't died, had I?

"No, I'm not going to give up and abandon Lessie. I'm not going to fall for these tricks." I didn't know if the spirits in the room with me really were my friends, but I couldn't give in. Even if Lessie wasn't waiting for me, there were still millions of innocent people at risk. Millions who would die if I didn't destroy the pieces of heart and stop the dragon god from being reborn.

Tavarian slowly rose from his chair. "Are you sure, Zara?" he asked, moving slowly toward me. With every step he took, his body grew more translucent, showing the bones beneath, the grinning skeleton. "You don't have to keep fighting. Just one sip of this, and you can stay here with us forever."

He held out a goblet of spiced wine, and the smell was so intoxicating, my knees buckled. *Damn you*, I snarled silently at myself. *Fight it!*

I knocked the goblet from his hand, and it sailed across the room. Dark red wine arced through the air like a spray of blood, and I jumped back as it splattered across the floor, unwilling to let a single drop touch me.

"Very well." Tavarian was stone-faced now, and my heart cried out at the sight of that implacable mask, the mask he only wore with strangers, with people he couldn't trust. "You may proceed. Goodbye, Zara."

"Tavarian—" I started, lunging forward to grasp his hand. But the room dissolved in a swirl of black smoke, and my fingers met only air. Hot tears trickled down my face, and I sincerely hoped that hadn't really been him. I couldn't bear it if I returned to the world of the living only to find out that he really was dead, and this really had been our last exchange.

When the world finally reformed around me, I stood on a narrow road. Tiny floating lights set along intervals illuminated the space barely enough to see the road stretched over a dark chasm. Faint screams sent icy chills racing down my spine as I walked, and I couldn't tell if the screams were coming from the chasm below or from something up ahead.

I kept walking forward, and eventually became aware of a faint light ahead. The air grew misty and humid as I approached; the light became large fires upon which huge black cauldrons perched. My stomach clenched at the sound of bubbling water laced with screams and sobs. The mist came from the great gouts of steam drifting from the cauldrons. There were three cauldrons total, and in the middle of them stood a behemoth of a man. He was completely naked except for the matted fur that covered his body. Well, most of his body. He had an unfortunate bald spot at the top of his head, and the fur didn't quite cover his manly bits.

"Aha!" the man cried as he laid eyes on me. He pointed the long wooden spoon at me, and for a minute I was afraid that he was about to scoop me up and toss me into one of the cauldrons. "You must be the new help. Took you long enough to arrive!"

"I, uh—"

"Don't you give me any lip. Derynnis promised me over a thousand years ago that he would send me an assistant, so you're beyond late! Go ahead and grab some logs from the pile over there. The fire's getting a little low on this one."

Wary, I skirted around the behemoth and headed for the log pile. Hefting as much wood as I could carry, I approached the cauldron with the lowest flame. Making a show of squatting down to pile the logs on, I ducked behind the side of the cauldron farthest from the man, then tossed my rope through the handle. Looping it through and tying a sturdy knot, I ignored the waves of heat rolling off the cauldron, then braced my foot against its side and climbed up until I was high enough to peer over the edge.

What I saw nearly made me lose my footing and fall into the fire.

"Help us!" the voices inside screamed. Hundreds of naked men and women flailed desperately inside the pot, trying to claw their way out. Their skin was lobster-red from the scalding water, and I could see places where the skin had been boiled away completely, revealing the aggravated flesh beneath. My stomach pitched, and it took everything I had not to hurl the contents of my stomach into the water. It was already bad enough these poor souls were being boiled. They didn't need to be smothered by the scent of vomit at the same time.

"Oi!" The brute turned toward me, his rough-hewn features twisted into a scowl. "What are you doing over there! I told you to stoke the fire!"

I glared at him. "So that I can help you boil people alive?"

The behemoth snorted. "They ain't alive," he said slowly, in that tone you used on people who'd been dropped on their heads as an infant. "They're dead, and this is the punishment Derynnis has set for them as penance for the terrible deeds they committed in life. Now either you help me mete out their sentence, or you can join them!"

"I don't care why they're in there," I snarled. "I'm not going to torture people. Killing in self-defense is one thing, or maybe even twisting an arm to get information if it'll save lives. But this is wrong no matter which way you put it!"

The giant roared in anger as he lunged for me. I dropped to the ground, barely avoiding his meaty hand as he tried to snatch me, then rolled to the side and slashed at his calf with my dagger. He roared with pain as blood gushed from the wound, and I rolled out of the way as he stomped with both feet, trying to flatten me.

"I'll skin you alive for this!" he shrieked, whirling around as he tried to find me. I darted between the cauldrons, round and round, forcing him to chase me in circles until he was dizzy. When I was certain he was sufficiently disoriented, I went back to the cauldron I'd climbed earlier, grabbed the rope, and raced between his legs.

"Gotcha!" His foot slammed into me, and I flew ten feet through the air before crashing to the ground. Searing pain ripped through my body as I struggled to my feet, and I gripped the dagger hard enough to leave an imprint on my palm, really hoping I wouldn't have to fall back on it.

The behemoth lunged for me, and unwittingly yanked the rope I'd just tied around his ankle. The cauldron lurched forward, and the giant let out a blood-curdling scream as a wave of scalding water crashed over him. The boiled men and women spilled out of the cauldron as well, and they wasted no time piling onto the giant, letting out war cries as they pummeled him with their fists. The giant tried to fight them, ripping the attackers off his body and flinging them against the wall, but there were too many, and he toppled to the ground, overwhelmed by the sheer numbers.

"ENOUGH!" a deep, male voice boomed, shaking the foundations of the platform we stood on. Everyone froze, even the naked people, and the giant's orange eyes nearly bugged out of their skull as he stared at something behind me.

"M-master," he sputtered, jabbing a finger at me. "I-I didn't—"

"Enough," the voice repeated, and an icy fist closed around me, squeezing my body until I could barely draw a breath.

"Get back to work, Grath. I will deal with this one now."

TWENTY-TWO

"Dammit!" I yelled, struggling against the giant hand as it pulled me back into the darkness. But I barely had time to fight before it let go, and my forward momentum sent me careening into what felt very much like a stone pillar. My forehead smacked against the hard stone, and I stumbled back, stars swimming in my vision.

"You do know this is a holy place, don't you?" the voice said as I let out a stream of curses. I turned toward the sound, one hand pressed against the swelling knot on my forehead, and my knees nearly gave out as I stared up at an enormous man sitting on a giant golden throne. Ancient golden eyes regarded me from a face as black as night, and I swallowed hard as we sized each other up. He had to be at least twenty feet tall, a massive giant with muscles stacked on top of muscles. I'd imagined him to be in black robes, like the specter who'd greeted me, but instead he wore a leather apron over a simple jerkin and trousers. The fanciest things he wore were the gloves—gold, emblazoned with strange fiery runes that shifted, making them impossible to read.

"Derynnis." Slowly, I sank to my hands and knees, as Caor had instructed me, and bowed until my forehead touched the swirling black and white marble floor. My heart hammered against my chest as the weight of his gaze pressed into my back. By refusing to stoke the flames, had I failed the test? Would Derynnis throw me out of his domain, or worse, trap me in one of the many hells he'd designed? "It is an honor."

"I would say so," he agreed, and there was a hint of amusement in his voice. "Rise, Champion. I have not brought you here to punish you. At least not today."

I cautiously got to my feet and looked around the room. We were no longer in that terrible place with the vats of boiling water, but in a spacious temple. Directly in front of me was Derynnis's throne, while to my left, several hundred yards away, a giant furnace burned. A hammer and anvil rested there, as well as a blacksmith's worktable and a variety of other tools. To my right was a stone arch that led to a starry landscape, and my breath caught at the sight of a large, swirling constellation hovering directly outside. Without thinking, I took a step toward it.

"I would not go that way if I were you." Derynnis's voice penetrated the haze of wonder that had enveloped my mind, and my gaze snapped back to his. Yes, there was no doubt about it—he found the little mortal in his temple amusing. "If you step through that gate you will find yourself in another world entirely, one where dragons do not exist."

That was enough to make my blood run cold. "'Thanks for

the warning," I said. "Now, did I pass the test, or are you going to send me back there and make me boil those people after all?"

Derynnis lifted a snow-white eyebrow at me. "You do not approve of my methods," he said.

"I don't generally approve of cooking people alive. Or dead," I added hastily when his other eyebrow rose. "In fact, I think cooking people is a waste of good water and firewood. Why do that when you can make a good trogla stew instead?"

Derynnis gave me a longsuffering sigh. "Your point would be valid if I were planning to eat the souls who are being cooked, but that is not the reason Grath is boiling them. Now," he said before I could argue further, "you can either argue with me about the morality of boiling serial rapists and murderers as penance for their crimes, or you can address the real reason you suffered through my trials to speak to me. I won't entertain both."

"Oh." That the people Grath boiled were such terrible humans made me feel better about leaving them in his care. "In that case, let's get right to it. But first, can I have my stuff back?"

Derynnis clapped his hands, and I once more wore my own clothes and weapons. Tugging on one of the pouches tied to my belt, I removed one of the two pieces of heart and held it up for Derynnis to see. The huge black diamond glittered in the firelight, and I suppressed a shudder as the dark, icy-cold energy coming from the relic began to seep into my skin.

"This is a piece of Zakyiar the Dragon God's heart," I told him. "I've brought two of them with me, and I need you to destroy them both."

Derynnis listened patiently as I told him about the pieces of heart and Salcombe's quest to resurrect the dragon god so he could lay waste to the world.

"Caor told me you are the only god powerful enough to destroy this," I said, holding up the relic again. "Please, Derynnis, if you have any care at all for what happens to this world, help me ensure that the dragon god can never again arise."

Derynnis's golden eyes glittered as he gently took the piece of heart from me. The diamond was huge, nearly as large as my head, and yet between the death god's thumb and forefinger it seemed no larger than an earring.

"Astonishing," he said as he examined it. "The properties of this jewel...I think if I cut it down a bit, it would fit the pommel of the blade I'm working on perfectly."

"Excuse me?" I wasn't sure I'd heard him right. "You want to use a piece of a bloodthirsty, world-destroying dragon god's heart as a decoration for a sword?"

Derynnis scowled. "Not for decoration, but to augment the sword's power." With a wave, a longsword appeared, floating above his massive palm. Even from where I stood, I could tell it was a beautiful piece, an elegant blade made of some kind of silvery metal that was definitely not of this world. Or at least that's what I assumed by the way it shimmered, reflecting colors I'd never seen before and wasn't sure I could ever accurately describe. The hilt was a work of art in itself, forged into some kind of intricate filigree pattern, with an empty setting in the center where a jewel should go.

"I didn't hand the relic over so you could use it to create some terrifying weapon," I said through gritted teeth. Beneath my anger, a current of bone-chilling fear coursed through my veins at the thought of a death god simply keeping the relic. The diamond was large enough to cut into enough pieces to make several swords. "What are you even going to do with that thing when you're done with it? Do you just keep it with your other swords as a collection?"

"Some," Derynnis said with a shrug. "Others are given to the gods, or even occasionally a mortal, though it is very rare to find one who has the mental and physical strength needed to wield one of my blades. Don't fret, child," he added a little crossly at the look on my face. "I wouldn't give this to a mortal from your world. It has been ages since one has been born who was worthy."

"Glad to hear it," I said, "but using the dragon heart pieces isn't the same as destroying them to make sure he can never be resurrected. What if Zakyiar just sends minions to steal the swords back? Either from here or from whoever you decide to gift them to in another realm?"

Derynnis snorted. "He barely has the strength to manipulate a handful of humans in your own realm." But he propped his chin on his massive fist and considered for a moment. "You have two pieces of the dragon god's heart, do you not?"

"I do." I pulled out the other one.

"Very well." He plucked that one out of my hand as well. "Then I will destroy this one and keep the other one for myself."

"But—"

He crushed the piece of heart between his thumb and forefinger before I could finish speaking, reducing the diamond into a cloud of glittering black dust. A deafening boom shook the temple as a blast of power rippled outward, and my amulet flared to life, protecting me from the blast even as it knocked me off my feet. A blinding pain tore through my ears as the blast deafened me, and I squeezed my eyes shut as the pressure on my temples threatened to crush my skull.

"My apologies," Derynnis said. I heard a loud creak, and then his giant hand covered me like a warm blanket. A gentle heat seeped through my body, and I sighed in relief as the pain vanished. "I forgot to take your fragility into account before I destroyed the relic."

"That's quite all right," I said shakily as he helped me to my feet. I glanced around, expecting to see bits of black diamond dust floating through the air, but there was nothing left, not a single trace. A great weight lifted off my chest, and I sucked in the first deep breath in what felt like ages. "I'm just glad you destroyed it."

"Of course. I am not like the other gods—I always keep my word." His ancient eyes fixated on the remaining relic in his other hand. "Now begone from my realm, mortal. You have overstayed your welcome."

He flicked his hand in an impatient wave, and an invisible force hit me dead center, sending me speeding toward the furnace. I braced myself, expecting to be incinerated on the spot, but I passed through the flames harmlessly and instead hit solid ground, sprawled just inside the cavern entrance, where I'd started.

I was back in the realm of the living once more.

"*Zara!*" Lessie cried, and I sobbed in relief as the bond between us surged back to life. "*Zara, what happened? I haven't been able to reach you in days!*"

"I'm all right!" I reached through the bond and wrapped myself around her in a mental hug. *"Derynnis destroyed the piece of heart. Are the others still there?"* I tried to get to my feet, but a loud rumble shook the cavern, knocking me to the ground again.

"They left with Drakis, like you asked," Lessie said. *"They didn't want to, but I forced them. But we've got bigger problems now, Zara. The volcano's been making strange noises for days, and now—"*

"It's going to explode," I finished, hauling myself to my feet again. I scrambled down the side of the ledge, wincing as the sharp rocks cut me but refusing to stop. I needed to get out of there and back to Lessie. *"How much time do we have?"*

"I don't know, but I imagine it's not much longer—" Lessie started, and then her voice was drowned out by another deafening rumble. Several boulders rolled down the side of the mountain, and I flattened myself against the sharp rocks to keep from getting hit. I breathed a sigh of relief as the tremor subsided, thinking I'd escaped the worst.

Then the foothold gave out beneath me.

TWENTY-THREE

A scream tore from my throat as I fell, clawing frantically for something, anything to cling to. But the part of the mountainside I'd been clinging to was too steep, and the mountain itself was completely barren, so there was nothing to break my fall, no branch for me to grasp, no bushes for me to tumble into, nothing but air and a long, long, long—

"Oof!" I landed on something hard and lumpy far sooner than I should have, then immediately slid sideways. Instinct kicked in and I flipped over, grasping the pommel of the leather saddle. "*Lessie?*" I cried as I hauled myself onto her back. I could barely see anything through the green miasma that surrounded us.

"*It's me.*" I could feel her lungs burning through the bond as she struggled to hold her breath, to ingest as little of the toxin as possible. A deafening boom shook the air, and I cried out as a flaming boulder shot past us, narrowly missing Lessie's wing. "*I *knew you weren't going to be able to make it back down, so I started flying the moment I sensed you."*

"Dammit, Lessie!" Tears of despair stung my eyes as she pushed us higher into the sky, clearing the noxious smoke. Her entire body trembled with the effort, and I knew she'd already ingested too much of the deadly air. "Why? You should have stayed—"

"At the bay, so I could wait for you to die?" she snapped. *"We're in this together, Zara. If you die, I die."*

Right. For a split second, I'd forgotten. I glanced back as the volcano erupted, spewing geyser after geyser of lava from the top. The hot rock spilled down the sides of the mountain and raced across the land, covering everything in a glowing red layer. If there was anything living there, it would be consumed, and if it had a soul, it would travel to Derynnis's domain to be judged and possibly punished.

"Thank you for saving me," I said quietly as we flew south, putting as much distance between us and that accursed island as possible. *"I would have died if you hadn't caught me."*

"I know," Lessie said. *"What happened in the Underworld, Zara? Did you do something to piss Derynnis off?"*

"On the contrary, I'm pretty sure I made his day." I thought of the way he'd gazed almost lovingly at the second dragon heart piece. "I think he just decided he'd had enough of living things camping out on the island. Even though the Hellmouth is technically part of the living, Derynnis considers it his domain."

"And he doesn't like living things in his domain," Lessie finished. She was silent for a minute, then added, *"You know, I think I can respect that."*

I laughed. *"Trust you to be sympathetic to the surliest god in the pantheon,"* I said, patting her neck.

We flew south for a little while, hoping to find a patch of land for Lessie to rest. As the minutes passed, I could feel her growing weaker as the toxin spread through her blood, and panic took root in my chest, making it difficult to breathe. What if we didn't find a place for Lessie to rest? What if we did, and she never got up again?

"Hang on, Lessie," I said, rubbing her scales and trying to sound encouraging. *"Just a few more minutes, and we'll find something."*

As my hope faded, a huge dragon dropped from the clouds ahead of us.

"Muza?" I cried, recognizing the enormous silver dragon immediately. So Tavarian was alive after all! Lessie bugled a cry of joy as he drew alongside her, using his giant shoulder to support her.

"He says to jump onto his back to lighten the load," Lessie said, sounding tired but grateful.

I immediately did as he said, settling between Muza's shoulder blades and gripping one of his giant spikes. *"How did he find us?"* I asked Lessie as Muza slid his left wing under Lessie's, partially supporting her weight.

"Tavarian sent him," she said as Muza steered us southeast. *"He says there is a safe place we can go where there is food, water, and a healer."*

We flew another thirty minutes before we finally found a place to rest. This island was little more than a strip of land, with hardly any vegetation and no game, but Muza caught some fish for Lessie. I quenched my thirst and filled my canteen from puddles of rainwater left from a recent storm.

"*Come on, Lessie,*" I said, gently coaxing her to lift her head. Muza had brought back a giant blue-finned fish nearly twice my size. "*You need to eat.*"

"*I'm so cold,*" she whispered, curling in on herself. Her body trembled, and I hugged her, wishing there was something I could do, some herb or drink I could give her to alleviate the pain.

Muza gently nudged me aside, then blew a thin stream of flame over Lessie. The heat seemed to revive her some, and she lifted her head long enough to eat the fish, then fell back into an exhausted sleep.

I wanted to stay up and watch over Lessie, but the toll from the past couple of days finally hit me, and with a gentle nudge from Muza, I curled up with her and fell asleep. For the first time in weeks, the two of us both slept deeply, no longer plagued by either Salcombe or the dragon god in our dreams. We should have both been rested and energized the next morning, but I woke up with a headache, and Lessie still had the chills.

"*Muza says the toxin needs to be flushed from my body,*" Lessie said as Muza gave her another flame bath. The heat seemed to give her a boost of energy as well as warmth, staving off the effects of the toxin. "*Apparently there is a dragon healer on the island where he lives who can heal me, but there is no way for her to get to us. We have to go to her.*"

"Okay. Do you think you can make it?"

She nodded grimly. "*I have to.*"

I mounted up on Muza again, and we continued east. For nine days we flew over the ocean, resting as often as we could on various islands, many of which were quite nice. If not for Lessie's flagging strength and the gradually worsening headaches that plagued me, it might have been a nice trip. We'd left the Underworld behind, but it seemed it hadn't quite left us. Death was a constant companion lurking over our shoulders, just waiting for one of us to let down our guard so it could strike.

"How much longer do we have?" I asked Lessie as we made camp on the fourteenth day. The headaches hadn't gotten worse, but a lethargy had spread through my body, making my limbs and eyelids heavy. *"Do you think we'll be there tomorrow?"*

"If we're lucky," Lessie said as we snuggled together by the roaring bonfire. Despite the sweltering heat of the tropical climate and the huge fire Muza had made, Lessie still shivered. *"I'm so tired, Zara,"* she whispered, sounding close to tears.

"Shhh." I stroked Lessie's hide and hummed a childhood nursery melody to soothe her. Muza came to sit by us, and he nuzzled Lessie as he wrapped one of his great wings around her, offering his own warmth. He matched my hum with a rumbling purr that soothed us both, and soon enough, we were both asleep.

When I woke up, the sun was shining brightly overhead, and Lessie's trembling had stopped. I glanced around for Muza to find he'd already risen. Probably fishing, I thought.

"Lessie, did Muza tell you where he was going?"

No answer.

"Lessie?" I raised the volume on my mental voice, but she didn't stir. Panic rose in my chest as I scrambled to my feet,

feeling along her neck for her pulse. It was there, but very faint, and the burst of motion took everything out of me. I collapsed to my knees in front of her, tears blinding my vision, but somehow, I found the strength to grasp her shoulder, to hold onto her with everything I had.

"*Lessie,*" I sobbed, shaking her as hard as I could. "*Lessie, please wake up. Please!*"

A shadow passed over us, blanketing everything in a dark fog. And then I knew no more.

To be continued...

Zara and Lessie's adventures will continue in Secret of the Dragon, Book 6 of the Dragon Riders of Elantia series. Make sure to join the mailing list so you can be notified of future release dates, and to receive special updates, freebies and giveaways! Sign up at www.jasminewalt.com.

Did you enjoy this book? Please consider leaving a review. Reviews help us authors sell books so we can afford to write more of them. Writing a review is the best way to ensure that the author writes the next one as it lets them know readers are enjoying their work and want more. Plus, it makes the author feel warm and fuzzy inside, and who doesn't want that? ;)

ABOUT THE AUTHOR

NYT bestseller JASMINE WALT is obsessed with books, chocolate, and sharp objects. Somehow, those three things melded together in her head and transformed into a desire to write, usually fantastical stuff with a healthy dose of action and romance.

Her characters are a little (okay, a lot) on the snarky side, and they swear, but they mean well. Even the villains sometimes. When Jasmine isn't chained to her keyboard, you can find her practicing her triangle choke on the mats, spending time with her family, or binge-watching superhero shows. Drop her a line anytime at jasmine@jasminewalt.com, or visit her at www.jasminewalt.com.

ALSO BY JASMINE WALT

Of Dragons and Fae

Promised in Fire

Forged in Frost

The Baine Chronicles Series:

Burned by Magic

Bound by Magic

Hunted by Magic

Marked by Magic

Betrayed by Magic

Deceived by Magic

Scorched by Magic

Fugitive by Magic

Claimed by Magic

Saved by Magic

Taken by Magic

The Baine Chronicles (Novellas)

Tested by Magic (Novella)

Forsaken by Magic (Novella)

Called by Magic (Novella)

Her Dark Protectors

Written under Jada Storm, with Emily Goodwin

Cursed by Night

Kissed by Night

Hidden by Night

Broken by Night

The Dragon's Gift Trilogy

Written under Jada Storm

Dragon's Gift

Dragon's Blood

Dragon's Curse

The Legend of Tariel:

Written as Jada Storm

Kingdom of Storms

Den of Thieves

Made in United States
Orlando, FL
16 July 2024